# THE FLOCK OF BA-HUI
## AND OTHER STORIES

# The Flock of Ba-Hui and Other Stories

by Oobmab

translated by
Arthur Meursault
and Akira

A Camphor Press book

Published by Camphor Press Ltd

83 Ducie Street, Manchester, M1 2JQ
United Kingdom

www.camphorpress.com

© 2020 Camphor Press.

ISBN     978-1-78869-186-4   (ePub)
         978-1-78869-187-1   (paperback)
         978-1-78869-188-8   (hardcover)

The moral right of the author has been asserted.

Set in 11 pt Linux Libertine

# Contents

# Foreword the First

CHINA, being outside Lovecraft's familiar comfort zone of eerie New England, rarely features within the Cthulhu Mythos. Aside from a handful of references to shifty Asiatic men that get mixed in with Lovecraft's usual descriptions of the immigrant stock that he felt had polluted his beloved corner of Northeast America, the only hint at how China plays a part within the Mythos are two brief mentions in "Beyond the Wall of Sleep" and *The Shadow Out of Time* of the cruel empire of Tsan-Chan that is to come three thousand years hence. While we await the coming of 5000 AD and our future cruel overlords (perhaps sooner if current trends have their way), one can only wonder what horrors, as yet undescribed by any sane or rational man, must be lurking in that vast land of soaring Tibetan mountains and Mongolian deserts.

Thankfully, the ever-creeping tentacles of modern technology that entwine our once-separate countries and cultures together in an increasingly frenzied summoning ritual for the inevitable AI gods that wish to creep backward and invade our present age have brought the writings of H.P. Lovecraft to wider audiences. Public-domain stories like "The Call of Cthulhu" and *The Shadow over Innsmouth* have now been translated into Chinese and disseminated widely, creating a whole new legion of fans ready to be warped and disturbed by Lovecraft's unique brand of fiction. The spread of Western weird fiction into Chinese could not have come at a more opportune moment. Despite the existing stereotypes of a highly controlled and creatively stagnant internet (which is admittedly true in many areas), China in fact has a healthy and burgeoning online-fiction scene, largely free of official censorship and state interference. Over 330 million people — or about one in four Chinese — read online novels, with the majority being *wuxia*-style historical romances. It's big business too: Tencent's online ebook arm, China Literature, raised HK$8.3 billion from its listing in Hong Kong and has a market value of around HK$90 billion. Websites like wuxiaworld.com feature Chinese online stories translated into English and other languages. China's online literary scene is composed of millions of independent creators, making the scene a breath of fresh air when compared to the digital versions of already established mainstream media titles that traditional publishing houses — both Western and Asian — continue to bank on.

And somewhere amid this chthonic sea of digital fiction, Lovecraftian tales of ancient races hiding in deep caves and cyclopean cosmic horrors waiting to mindlessly consume us have also gained a foothold. The Ring of Wonder, which can be found at https://trow.cc/, has been a home for Chinese-language weird fiction since its inception in 2005. This website is where my fellow translator Akira found the online author "Oobmab" and his fantastic "The Flock of Ba-Hui."

"The Flock of Ba-Hui" plants itself firmly within the

Cthulhu Mythos, though since China lacks a tradition of horror writing it has precious little other choice. China, despite its lengthy history, has a literary tradition that perhaps pales in comparison when held up against, say, Victorian England or Tsarist Russia. When Chinese bring up the four great novels — *Journey to the West*, *Romance of the Three Kingdoms*, *The Water Margin*, and *A Dream of the Red Chamber* — these works stand out precisely because there are only four of them. Many of China's writers throughout its history were forced by the imperial examination system to devote themselves to dreary and repetitive poems and essays — essential for entering bureaucracy but hardly the most creative of enterprises. There are, of course, some exceptions. The Qing dynasty *Tales from the Liaozhai Studio* by Pu Songling is sometimes regarded as the main example of pre-modern Chinese horror writing, but these often quaint stories of fox fairies and hungry ghosts are more akin in style to Aesop's *Fables* or the Brothers Grimm than to something from a Poe or a Lord Dunsany. Luckily for us, the Chinese are adept at taking the best of other cultures and implanting it within their own traditions, the result being "The Flock of Ba-Hui" among others. Though this tale is set within the wild mountains of Sichuan, its style and pace would not be unfamiliar to those unfortunate residents of Arkham or Innsmouth.

The eagle-eyed reader of Lovecraft on the lookout for Easter eggs will find much to enjoy in "The Flock of Ba-Hui." Yig — Lovecraft's own snake-god creation — gets a namedrop, and the reader is left wondering if the serpentine Ba-Hui and his American cousin Yig could be one and the same. The tale involves a group of academics wandering through the fabulous remains of an ancient and lost civilization. Although the professors in this story don't hail from the Chinese campus of Miskatonic University, their exploits would certainly resonate with those unfortunate adventurers who explored subterranean caverns in *At the Mountains of Madness*. What our Chinese explorers find in those deep underground caves also bears more than a passing resemblance to the creatures and murals of "The Nameless City," not to mention the terrors lurking under Delapore's ancestral estate in "The Rats in the Walls."

We have selected three more of Oobmab's stories to present here, which in total provide an homage to Lovecraft's entire spectrum. Like "The Flock of Ba-Hui," these stories have us either descending into subterranean abysses or ascending into the starry realms of the infinite.

The less horrific and more fantastical tales featured in Lovecraft's Dream Cycle are given due respect in the short tale "Nadir." The only story in this short collection that isn't based in China, "Nadir" instead takes us on a journey through many locations from the Dream Cycle — Ooth-Nargai, Dylath-Leen, Sona-Nyl — while at the same time presenting a unique story that contemplates the nature of existence and eternity. The third story, "Black Taisui," is set in Qingdao — the picturesque Chinese coastal city that was formerly a German colony — and features an old friend who will be more than familiar to Lovecraft fans. Finally, "The Ancient Tower" brings us all the way to the lonely mountains of Tibet, where a typically Lovecraftian protagonist unleashes more than he bargained for when exploring ancient mysteries. The translators have also included a small story of their own creation to link the four main stories together — an idea concocted after overdosing on one too many portmanteau horror anthologies.

To some more cynical readers, the above synopses may sound a little too much within the Lovecraftian oeuvre, and there may be accusations of imitation. However, those cynics would do well to remember that in many ways Lovecraft's greatest legacy was not just the wonderful stories he left behind but the entire shared universe that he opened up to other writers to collaborate in and enjoy. Lovecraft was the first open-source programmer. Not only did he take elements of existing horror stories, like the style of Lord Dunsany or tropes from Robert W. Chambers' *The King in Yellow*, and make them his own, he also invited other writers to build on the ideas he personally created. Many of Lovecraft's works were collaborations with other authors, including "The Curse of Yig" which was written together with Zealia Bishop and is where the aforementioned snake-god Yig first reared his bestial head. After his death, other writers built upon the existing Mythos created by Lovecraft with his blessing, most notably August Derleth and Robert Bloch, who it could be argued did more to build the concept of Lovecraft's vision than the socially awkward Lovecraft did himself. The amateur Chinese authors at the Ring of Wonder are only continuing Lovecraft's wish for others to follow the path he pioneered, even if he may have deemed them of dubious racial stock, coming as they do from beyond the civilized borders of Providence.

We encourage those who can read Chinese to explore further stories set within the Cthulhu Mythos; there are some fantastic examples online that deserve to be translated and shown before a wider audience. At the very least it will fill the void while we all still await the definitive English translation of Abdul Alhazred's *Necronomicon* to be finally published.

*Iä! Iä! Cthulhu fhtagn!*

— Arthur Meursault is a long-term expat in Asia and amateur translator of Chinese. He is also the author of the China-based dark comedy *Party Members*, published by Camphor Press in 2016.

# Foreword the Second

WHAT is there to say?

I began this endeavor solo in December 2013. Having just finished a rewarding three years of intensive Chinese language study for my employment, I attempted to synthesize a recently acquired passion — for I hadn't even gotten into Lovecraft's oeuvre until a few months previously — with the skillset of which I found myself in possession. And behold, there online in the cubic and arcane corners of the internet — one strange forum known as the Ring of Wonder — lay reams of Lovecraftian fan fiction written exclusively in Chinese, fawned over by uncountable and obscure readers, waiting patiently (even timelessly) to be discovered by someone from outside the national wall of fire and transposed into a language of simpler graphemes. Oobmab was a singularly enthusiastic and helpful contact throughout this process, responding promptly to all of my questions. The initial effort proved insurmountably difficult for me, and after a valiant forty percent or so of translation completed on the initial short story, "The Flock of Ba-Hui," I abandoned the project — that is, until years later, when I made the effort a public affair. One imagines Oobmab tapping his foot to dust by this point.

Publicizing the translation of "The Flock of Ba-Hui"

was a twofold attempt at both hyping myself up for the completion of the story and holding myself account-able to complete it, lest I disappoint a large audience of people I respect. This gambit proved ten times more successful than I anticipated, when none other than Arthur Meursault contacted me via direct message to assist in the translation of the remainder of the work. And the rest is history. It seems my gusto for Lovecraft outpaced my capacity for Chinese, particularly in the wake of my move back to the English-speaking world. Maybe if I had stayed in Taipei, sipping Irish coffee in Kafka-by-the-Sea and watching sunsets from the Jin-lutian Temple — built, legend tells, inside a meteorite crater, at the end of a road that has long been sealed off from all but the most dedicated sojourners. These are real places; visit them.

Arthur, of course, took the entire affair one step fur-ther — with his own experience writing and publishing books he smelled the potential for a real production. He translated three more full stories from scratch and for some reason elected me worthy of a second pass over them for the "injection of flavor." What you are about to read is the result of our combined efforts and, of course, Oobmab's initial genius. Where possible we have attempted to preserve the poetry of the original text. Actually, an interesting aside: Oobmab's Chinese style is distinct because he has somehow replicated Love-craft's unique effect via purely Chinese grammatical and semantic mechanisms, which, in a language as nuanced as Chinese, is no small task. The effect is accomplished via layers of subordinate clauses that extend sentence lengths, along with not-quite-random walks through the semantic space adjacent to the relevant adjectives (which are rarely the same twice). It was unclear whether a direct translation of these mechanisms or a transposition of their intent to more English-native prose was the more faithful interpretation; please be satisfied with an admixture of both. The process of twisting the semantic content of these phrases into English has been an inextricable blend of the enjoyable and the excruciating.

— Akira, among many other things, tweets at @0xa59a2d about neoreaction and our inevitable dystopian future. He also assists the machine-god colonization of the human auditory noosphere at https://lovecrypt.bandcamp.com.

THE FLOCK OF BA-HUI
AND OTHER STORIES

The dull light of a table lamp flickered dimly as I whispered in the darkness to my nervous guests. Four of them there were, gathered from different cities of this land called China, but equally all men of great learning and standing.

It was my habit to seek out such men in order to learn from them some of the arcane mysteries that lie out of sight beyond the normal range of human knowledge. Such men were the keys to the gates of perception, though in many cases they were too ignorant or frightened to realize just how deep into the universe's great cosmic obscurities they had truly penetrated. More often than not they needed a guide who could usher them through the dark hallways of horrors from beyond, someone akin to the psychopomps of legend, who would escort the spirits of the dead down into the depths of the eternal afterlife.

For this purpose I had gathered them here to this abandoned farmhouse in the desolate regions of western China. Here among the remote Himalayan foothills — in the deep woods of the highest peaks, and the shadowy valleys where streams trickle from faraway sources — I had brought them. These men were from the bustling metropolises of the eastern coast — from crowded Beijing or scenic Qingdao, where ample light and fellow man kept at bay the obscene terrors that haunt the night in more isolated regions. Yet in this part of China, secrets were still to be found lurking in the wild mountain ranges or in forgotten caves buried beneath the desert. We were far away from the mechanized, urbanized coastal and southern regions — an unspoiled ancestral China without the foreigners, factory smoke, billboards, and concrete roads of those provinces that modernity has devoured. Here, in this lonely farmhouse nestled between daemonic hills, we could share our secrets.

Of my guests, I was familiar with their individual backgrounds and their discoveries, though it was my personal habit to disregard names during these sessions and instead refer to each visitor by a more befitting sobriquet. Based on their stories, I had temporarily bestowed on them the following names: the Researcher, the Dreamer, the Historian, and the Anthropologist. Our room was a simple study of modest construction; my guests were positioned at one end of the room, while I sat at the opposite end, little more than a table and lamp between us. I had deliberately chosen the middle of the night and dimmed the lights, as was my habit, bright light being unconducive to my thought processes when engaged in deep contemplation.

Other than my guests and the aforementioned table, there was precious little furniture in the room other than a large wooden box that I had placed before my person. This box was of great antiquity and decorated with peculiar and indecipherable symbols of an occult and blasphemous nature, but far more of interest were the objects lying within. Each one of these objects had a connection to my individual guests, and it was my purpose in inviting them here to learn more about the inscrutable histories behind these objects and whatever information about those antediluvian times from before the ascent of man they could impart. This land was an old land; a land of countless dynasties and kingdoms rising and falling, of barbarian hordes rampaging from the north and west, of dusty oracle bones and stone warriors buried in cavernous tombs. Yet these were mere novelties compared to the true antiquities that lay hidden in obscure corners far, far away from the trivial politics of Beijing. Few realize just how far back the real history of this land extends — back to dark primordial eons when our remote ancestors peered out in fright from burrows and treetops.

I reached into the box and pulled out the first object: an unbelievably ancient scroll of ashen grey that emitted such a heavy sense of age that I felt I was almost holding dust from the very moment of earth's creation. I have had the pleasure of reading many of this planet's oldest and most diabolical works, not least the hideous and abhorred Necronomicon, whose weathered pages bore more than a passing resemblance to the aged leathery scroll I now held; but this artefact disturbed me for unknown reasons that I could not fathom. The symbols on the scroll — written in a brown ink like long-dead blood — seemed to brood as I cast my gaze over their strange and angular curves. I was familiar with most of the East Asian languages and scripts, yet I had never before seen hieroglyphs in this style. All I could say for certain was that it was indubitably unrelated to the Sinitic languages, though its origin was supposedly here in the far western regions of China.

The scroll had been in the possession of the one I had named the Researcher, and it was to him that I now turned as I held up the ancient scroll.

"Tell me more of this scroll and its meaning. I wish to

know more about what it contains and the circumstances that surround your connection to it."

The Researcher was reluctant to speak initially — a reaction quite understandable given the situation but one that I could not permit to endure. The Researcher knew of my capabilities — as I rose to my feet and glowered in his direction, the Researcher began to speak.

"It is from Sichuan," said the Researcher. "From deep within the mountains, where dark caverns pierce into the bowels of the earth and no man has trodden for millennia. Its roots lie with Ba-Hui, and the flock that worships him."

"Ba-Hui?" I replied. I sat back down and waved the Researcher to proceed further. Mercifully, I did not need to impose myself before the Researcher again; he dutifully began to recite the strange tale of that gnarled parchment and the being known as Ba-Hui, which slithered and wormed its way into all the aspects of this story....

The others listened too; we all did. Outside, the moon rose higher in the sky, and only the occasional sound of an animal rustling in the undergrowth disturbed the perfect quiet of the night.

# The Flock of Ba-Hui

# Introduction

Five years ago, Zhang Cunmeng, a post-doctoral researcher at the Sichuan Cultural Anthropology Institute and a good friend of mine, escaped from the Humane Mental Hospital of Chengdu and vanished without a trace. The date was May 24.

Most people won't have heard of this, of course, but his disappearance caused quite a stir in academic circles. Just before being diagnosed with the severe anxiety that prompted his admittance to the mental institution, Zhang had announced his discovery of a once-flourishing prehistoric civilization — somehow absent from modern archaeological knowledge — in southwest Sichuan Province. A few sensationalists believed that his mental episode and sudden disappearance were a publicity stunt, carefully crafted to redeem his academic reputation. Others believed that the "new discovery" was a delusion of his insanity, and his disappearance only further illustrated the extent of his incurable condition.

Zhang's most frequent contacts had a different perspective. They maintained that Zhang's advancing neurological problems prevented him from publishing his eccentric, but genuine, research on the ancient civilization. However, even his few sympathizers had to concede that his surviving materials, although consistent, were scattered and lacking in substantial evidence. In order to bear out his life's work, a few of Zhang's truest supporters organized a private investigation in the hopes of uncovering some workable proof — and I, your author, chose to join them. I would soon wish I never had. The results of the investigation were never released to the public.

Last month, the People's Court of Qingyang district proclaimed Zhang Cunmeng deceased after being missing for one year. His family was to hold a symbolic funeral procession in his honor. Upon hearing the news, I immediately bought a ticket to Chengdu to attend the simple ceremony with a few of his former research associates — together for the first time since concluding our expedition. We did not mention the investigation during the funeral. Our monstrous discovery would only have made the others more suspicious. Besides, on occasions like that, some things are better left unsaid. Despite our ten-year friendship with Zhang, despite everything we'd done for the investigation and our vow to never to speak of it again — we had lost him for eternity.

I often wonder whether Zhang is still alive. Although it terrifies me to imagine the unspeakable fate that may have befallen him, I cannot resist the morbid allure of this unbanishable nightmare. For years I followed the trail of breadcrumbs that he had left behind, feverishly studying anything I could get my hands on. Much of the best evidence had been lost along with his original work, and I labored tirelessly to assemble what had really happened from the pieces of what remained. With time, even I lost track of what was truth and what was wild hallucination.

My few friends from that expedition are content to let sleeping beasts lie, but I cannot bear to leave our incomparable discoveries — and what could have been Zhang's own revelations — in the dark. Science, and history, must record what we have learned, no matter how dire its portent. I will tell the whole story, from hard facts to bizarre conjecture, both to settle my mind and to provide a new perspective on Zhang's disappearance — and the glimpse we witnessed of endless time.

# PART ONE
# The Story of Zhang Cunmeng

It started in the spring of 2007. That March, Zhang was invited to attend a conference at Boston University, thanks to a Chinese–American archaeological research agreement. In Boston, he met one Dr. David J. Whitener, a researcher of East Asian culture at the Cabot Museum, which at the time was holding a special exhibition on Far Eastern relics. Sensing a rare opportunity, Dr. Whitener invited Zhang to have a look around the museum after the conference concluded. The definitive circumstances of the visit are lost to the ages, as such a fleeting event is naturally impossible to investigate, but in his unsteady handwriting, Zhang made repeated (almost rambling) notes of a singular artefact — a leather scroll of unknown origin.

I emailed Dr. Whitener once about this affair. The kind-hearted old man enthusiastically corroborated my reconstructed version of the events, and also sent me a few pictures of the leather scroll. After a cautious examination of the photographs, I had to agree with Zhang: the peculiar artefact was at once eye-catching and thoroughly incomprehensible. I could make neither head nor tail of it.

The leather hide was extremely old, appearing to have undergone an extraordinary artisanal tanning technique for swine-skin. Its carefully trimmed edges were about six inches wide by twelve long, and the whole thing was a dead, pallid grey. What disturbed me, however, lay in the center of that ashen parchment: a striking sequence of symbols, smeared in an unusual dark-brown ink. The symbols seemed at first glance to be oracle bone, or perhaps bronze inscription-style characters — not uncommon for ancient Far Eastern artefacts — but after careful examination, one discovered these symbols originated from an altogether separate codex. Nevertheless, frequent students of archaeology can readily recognize an ideographic system. Altogether there were seventy of these symbols, neatly arranged in five rows by fourteen columns, repeating only rarely — hinting that the ancient tongue was complex indeed.

Dr. Whitener also sent me some information about the scroll's history. According to the museum archives, the relic had been brought to America by an explorer named Claude Jacobs in the 1920s, who traded for it in a remote village somewhere near the current border of

Sichuan Province. Mr. Jacobs wrote in great detail of his dealings with the villagers in bartering for the leather scroll, noting that it had been originally preserved in "an especially disgusting little mud pot, whose surface was etched with a pattern of obscene deities." Sadly, by the time Cabot's grandson Thomas bequeathed Mr. Jacob's expansive collection of curios to the Cabot Museum in 1986, only the scroll remained. The pot had been lost.

The scroll was unnaturally thin but, although it came from a distant era, had retained the soft suppleness of skin. No doubt some uniquely powerful process had tanned it. So far there was no consensus on exactly to which species of animal the skin belonged. Having exchanged hands many times, the leather's carbon was quite severely contaminated, preventing the Cabot Museum from evaluating it with carbon-14 dating. More-over, due to lacking a similar artefact to reference, the museum was unable to pinpoint the leather scroll's precise era. On top of that, deciphering the symbols proved an ordeal worthy of Sisyphus. Claude Jacobs had originally thought the symbols to be primitive Tibetan, but Tibetan scholars quickly eliminated this possibility. The museum had already sent a transcript to the most prominent linguists and archeo-graphologists of the day, but not one of them could decrypt it — or even locate a similar specimen.

What had stood out most to Dr. Whitener was Zhang's miraculous understanding of the inscrutable object. In his email, Dr. Whitener wrote that upon studying the scroll, Zhang was able to offer him a new perspec-tive. During an expansive excavation of the ruins of Sanxingdui (the "Three Stars Mound") in April 2005, the

Paleoanthropological Institute of Sichuan had unearthed an unusual bronze statue of a snake. It was more or less a common Sanxingdui artefact by design, but its decoration made it exceptional: the partial statue had been carved over and over with a single strange mark, the like of which had not yet been observed on any known artefact. Zhang, having studied the odd bronze snake before, dimly recognized the hints of likeness between that symbol and the dark handwritten characters of the leather scroll. Since the scroll had been discovered in a village on the district border, Zhang inferred it must have originated in either the plains of Chengdu or a remote corner of the mountains of western Sichuan.

Naturally, this new perspective captivated Dr. Whitener. He gave Zhang several high-resolution photos of the scroll and brought him to the museum's archives for access to Claude Jacobs' microfilm journal entries. According to Dr. Whitener, Zhang spent over two hours taking copious notes at that tiny viewing screen, and fought to stay longer when the time came for the museum to close. He had to be escorted, brokenhearted, from the archive room. Zhang promised Dr. Whitener he would return to the States to continue researching the matter, and to follow the gossamer-thin threads in Jacobs' journal to settle the question of the scroll's origin once and for all. Regrettably, although the two of them kept in contact, it seemed that Zhang's research — and their correspondence — eventually slowed to a crawl, until the whole affair faded almost completely from Dr. Whitener's memory. Indeed, until I reached out to him, Dr. Whitener had not even heard of Zhang's disappearance.

Even working alone, Zhang managed to uncover more information about the leather scroll. Lab records indicate that between March and August of 2008, he conducted three large-scale investigations in Sichuan's southwestern mountains, covering Ya'an, Garze, and the three cities of Liangshan. The few pages remaining in the archives sketch only a rough picture of this period. What is blindingly clear, by contrast, is that he not only somehow located the Yi tribal village[1] that Claude Jacobs once visited, but he personally interviewed a council of septuagenarian elders who still recognized the leather scroll in his painstaking diagrams.

The elders called it the "*zi suo mo*." The name meant nothing in the Yi dialect — it was a loan word from another language. The ancient villagers told Zhang it meant "exuvium of the dragon" or "dragon's shedded skin," which was obviously a metaphor passed down in oral tradition. They did not know how the scroll had been treated, nor the animal from whence it came. One often heard similarly clouded tales to explain artefacts of unknown origin in other corners of southern Sichuan. The myths were more ancient than even Jumu Wuwu;[2] nobody knew whence or from whom they originated. In

1    The Yi people are a minority ethnic group of China who are also found in Thailand and Vietnam. They live primarily in the rural areas of Sichuan, Yunnan, Guizhou, and Guangxi, usually in mountainous regions. Their language is closely related to Burmese.

2    Jumu Wuwu is a character in an old Yi legend about a great flood. In the legend, Jumu Wuwu is the only person to survive the great flood, by hiding in a wooden box.

legend, the *zi suo mo* was a certificate of mountain-, or perhaps earth-godhood — received from one, or possibly made by one — granting the bearer transcendence from mortality, along with the ability to enter the subterranean realm of the mountain gods. The painted symbols on the scroll belonged to the gods' grotesque script.

I recognized the importance of this information and sought a way to find that Yi village. I studied the traditions and legends of the surrounding towns intensely, but the results of my research only cast me deeper into despair. It seemed that the inexorable millstone of time had ground any myths surrounding the *zi suo mo* to dust, leaving only specious fragments of half-truth behind. Mercifully, however, there was one legend favored by the Yi that had, through many retellings, gradually blended into the folktales of their everyday lives, concealing its grains of truth among the sands of time.

For several reasons, I've included the complete story below. It hints ever so slightly at ... something, and might assist me in explaining better what I must tell you happened next.

* * *

It is said that before ancient times, humankind did not know fraternity, and tribespeople slew their kindred. There were six brothers who sought shelter from their murderous foes among the tall mountains, although they knew not the hardships of life among the treacherous peaks.

One day, the eldest of the six brothers went hunting deep within the mountain range. He walked over many summits, climbing finally to the timeless southern peaks of Mount Nanyu[3] until he could walk no more, and collapsed, weeping at the entrance to a cliffside cave.

Soon, the spirit of Mount Nanyu heard the sound of weeping and appeared inside the cave, asking: "Why do you choose to weep here?"

The eldest brother said: "O mountain spirit, why must the mountains be so tall? We walk until we grow tired. Wilt thou not flatten this precipice into a plain?"

The spirit of Mount Nanyu answered him: "This I cannot do, but I shall make you tall and strong, for to carry your brothers over the high mountains." So the eldest brother thanked the mountain spirit, and he returned to tell his brothers what he had experienced that day.

On the second day, the second brother came to the cliffside cave and began to weep. Soon, the spirit of Mount Nanyu heard the sound of weeping and appeared inside the cave. The second brother said: "O mountain spirit, why must the wolf's sight be so sharp? He attacks me before I know he is there. Why must the deer's ears be so clever? He eludes

3   Mount Nanyu is a legendary mountain in Chinese mythology mentioned in *The Classic of Mountains and Seas*. It was said to be the home of many divine creatures, including dragons and snakes with human heads.

me before I can capture him. Wilt thou not cloud the wolf's eyes to blind him to me, and stuff the deer's ears to deafen him to me?"

The spirit of Mount Nanyu answered him: "This I cannot do, but I shall make your ears clear and your vision bright. This way, you shall hear the wolf before he discovers you and see the deer's tracks before he hears you." So the second brother also thanked the mountain spirit, and he returned to tell his brothers what he had experienced that day.

On the third day, the third brother came to the cliffside cave and began to weep. Soon, the spirit of Mount Nanyu heard the sound of weeping and appeared inside the cave. The third brother said: "O mountain spirit, why must the jackals, wolves, tigers, and panthers have their claws to strike, and jaws to bite and kill me, while I have not a thing? Wilt thou not dull their claws and pluck their fangs?"

The spirit of Mount Nanyu answered, "This I cannot do, but I shall make your teeth grow sharp and your legs grow long. This way, you shall drive them all out." So the third brother also thanked the mountain spirit, and he returned to tell his brothers what he had experienced that day.

On the fourth day, the fourth brother came to that cliffside cave with his wife and children and began to weep. Soon, the spirit of Mount Nanyu heard the sound of weeping and appeared inside the cave. The fourth brother and his family said: "O mountain spirit, why must our children grow so slowly? They cannot hunt alongside our brothers. Wilt thou not make our children grow, to help us make a living together?"

The spirit of Mount Nanyu answered, "This I cannot do, but your tribe must bear children to survive. Return to your brothers, and tell them I have bidden you never to hunt and hence only care for the children of the tribe." So the fourth brother and his family also thanked the mountain spirit, and they returned to tell his brothers what he had experienced that day.

On the fifth day, the fifth brother came to the cliffside cave and began to weep. Soon, the spirit of Mount Nanyu heard the sound of weeping and appeared inside the cave. The fifth brother said: "O mountain spirit, why must life in the mountains be such hardship? Wilt thou not make the fruits pick themselves from the trees, and the animals yield themselves to slaughter, that we might never work nor suffer again?"

The spirit of Mount Nanyu answered, "This I cannot do, but you may return to your brothers and tell them that I have bidden you never to work again, and they shall take half of what they glean and give it to you." So the fifth brother also thanked the mountain spirit, and he returned to tell his brothers what he had experienced that day.

On the sixth day, the sixth brother came to that cliffside cave and began to call out the name of the spirit of Mount Nanyu. Soon, the spirit of Mount Nanyu heard the shouting and appeared inside the cave.

The spirit of Mount Nanyu said to him, "Your five brothers have already come to me and made their demands; and why have you come?" The sixth brother simply said: "O mountain spirit, thank you for your willingness to help my brothers. But wilt thou not always remain here to protect us?"

The spirit of Mount Nanyu answered him, "This I cannot do, but I shall teach you enough to guide your brothers to live on the mountain forever." Taking his hand, the spirit of Mount Nanyu gave unto the sixth brother the knowledge of calendars, rituals, and sacrifice, and then disappeared into the mountain cave.

When the seventh day came, the promises of the mountain spirit all came true. The eldest brother grew tall and strong, tall as the pines when he stood, his hands wide as canyons; so he carried all of the brothers over ridges, peaks, and valleys to level ground. The second brother grew the eyes of the wolf and the ears of the deer, so he led his brothers to find prey, and away from danger. The third brother grew the claws and teeth of a tiger, so he killed the prey for his brothers and drove away the beasts of the mountain. The fourth brother and his family bore many more children and nurtured them, to the joy and prosperity of the tribe. The fifth brother received the boon of the mountain spirit, and the others gave unto him half of all that was theirs, that he might never work again. The sixth brother mastered the calendric knowledge of the spirit of Mount Nanyu and helped his brothers manage the sacrificial rites of the gods of earth and sky.

After one cycle of the calendar of the mountain god, the spirit of Mount Nanyu emerged once again from his cliffside cave. The sixth brother had bidden his brothers to go and sacrifice, but they said: "We work all day long but make no surplus; how then shall we make tribute?" The sixth brother saw the sense in this, so he feasted and spent the day in rest, treating the others' offerings to the fifth brother as tribute to the mountain spirit. The spirit of Mount Nanyu saw that the fifth brother grew hideously fat, living easy off the sacrifice of his five brothers.

Then the spirit of Mount Nanyu taught the sixth brother to make the *zi suo mo*, for to bring their sacrifices once more to the cliffside cave. The sixth brother crafted the *zi suo mo*, and he became the new spirit of the mountain, to bless and protect his brothers to live on the mountain forever.

\* \* \*

Obviously, the folktale elucidated the origins of that mysterious scroll to an extent. Ours was without a doubt the *zi suo mo* of the Yi people, but the myth itself had revealed more troubling unknowns. I contacted my friends in the folklore research department for a discussion, and they informed me in no uncertain terms that this fable traced its origins to the far-flung recesses of time immemorial. The most immediate evidence would be its faint hints at the rituals of the time ... that is, the act of sacrificing one's brother to the mountain gods.

No, it was no act of martyrdom. As a consecration of heaven and earth, the people of the Central Plain once offered up the lives of their fellow tribesmen in sacrifice. This tradition supposedly ended long ago; the most recent example dated back to the Dongyi graves of the Western Zhou period.[4] Although there was no consensus on exactly when ancient Sichuan witnessed these human sacrifices, it could not have taken place later than King Huiwen of Qin's conquest of the region[5]. This fable, if accurate, could represent three thousand years of history. Zhang had no doubt learned of this myth too — he had asked a friend of mine, also a scholar of southwestern customs, about a very similar story back in the autumn of '07. This, among other reasons, may have been why he chose to name his prehistoric discovery "The Old Country of Nanyu."

At any rate, the fable yielded no other useful information. It held only fragments of fragments, making further inductions impossible to extract. Anyone else would

4    1027–771 BC.

5    338–311 BC.

have believed they had hit a dead end. Fortunately — or unfortunately — Zhang had a knack for the names of ancient places. He discovered his next clue submerged in an ocean of ancient books: a scarcely mentioned peak once known as "Mount Nanyu."

It was not long before academic circles heard the news. In October 2008, Zhang held a conference in Beijing titled "Origins of China's Ancient Civilizations," at which he first announced his discovery of the "ancient country of Nanyu." His report sparked such an intense debate that his critics spent most of the cross-examination period contradicting his findings. Although I did not make it to that summit, when I first heard his thesis I could already imagine the outrage it would provoke.

Due to a lack of concrete evidence for his hypotheses, Zhang had understandably resorted to citing ancient texts as reference. His error, however, was grave. Most of the documents he quoted were not trusted historical records but supernatural texts: among them were Wang Jia's *Forgotten Tales of the Eastern Jin*,[6] Liu An's *Masters of Huainan of the Western Han*,[7] and the more doubtful *Tale of King Mu, Son of Heaven*.[8] This was not to mention the apocrypha that most of academia considered to be

6    Wang Jia lived during the Eastern Jin period of 317–420 AD. The book is a collection of supernatural events and stories.

7    The Western Han dynasty existed from 206 BC to 8 AD. Liu An was king of Huainan, and the book is a record of a series of scholarly debates held at his court.

8    A fantasy version of the travels taken by King Mu of the Zhou dynasty from around 950 BC.

counterfeits, some so obscure even I had never heard of them: the four scrolls of the *Kunlun Scriptures*[9] in the *Classic of Mountains and Seas*,[10] the unfathomable *Seven Cryptical Books of Hsan*,[11] and finally the *Records of the Great Wilderness*,[12] a forbidden scroll that once drove an emperor to try to burn every copy in existence. Evidence of this sort was, charitably, hard to believe. At worst, it demonstrated that the so-called ancient country of Nanyu was nothing but an indulgent, fantastical prank.

But the general consensus did not sway everyone. A small minority of researchers noticed that the calm, careful, and holistic consultation of the pseudepigrapha had revealed a bizarre phenomenon: although the old texts had been written in vastly different eras and locations, their contents — especially concerning Ancient Nanyu — were unusually consistent, with the most detailed myths found in the *Records of the Great Wilderness*, of the Qin dynasty. The accounts of the *Records*, specifically the folktales from Nanyu, seemed to upset people considerably, eliciting thoughts of dread, directionless horror, and lasting nightmares in at least one case. According to these accounts, the mountains of ancient southwestern

9   The author is making a joke here: *Kunlun Scriptures* is the name of a television show.

10  A real book dating from China's earliest recorded history, it is a fantastical encyclopedia of mythical geography, animals, herbs, and legends.

11  Mentioned in Lovecraft's "The Other Gods" and *The Dream-Quest of Unknown Kadath*.

12  One of the books that make up the *The Classic of Mountains and Seas*.

Sichuan once held an incomparably powerful empire that had flourished in glory for hundreds, even thousands of generations — before the formation of modern-day China, before the civilizations of ancient Sichuan, and even before the first primitive tribesman set foot in those Neolithic mountains.

According to the tome, the inhabitants of that land were called the Yu-Hui, possibly the original settlers of the southwestern plains. When the book was written, Nanyu had already developed into a fiercely prosperous empire, although there was no mention of when it had originated. From the central mountains across to the vast southern range, Nanyu held the entirety of the Bashu plains in its power. In its later years of decline, war broke out between it and the developing nation of ancient Shu.[13] To bring an end to the conflict, the Nanyu empire agreed to relinquish the Bashu plains while retaining its home among the mountains, so long as the Shu paid annual tribute to preserve a peaceful equilibrium. The two states honored this pact for almost a thousand years. It was possible that a small amount of Nanyu mythology, tradition, and religion had been passed down to the ancient Shu, and finally, osmoted into China's own.

Religion held immense sway in that old empire. Unlike other early East Asian civilizations, the Yu-Hui worshipped neither nature nor totems; these mysterious inhabitants of antiquity revered only a single deity and its offspring. The god was known as "Ba-Hui,"[14] or the

13  Modern-day Sichuan.
14  "Ba" relates to an old name for Sichuan Province; "Hui" is a putative, legless dragon.

"Great Serpent." The Yu-Hui believed Ba-Hui was unimaginably gargantuan, its body sunken beneath the Four Seas and coiling around the eight cardinal directions, encircling every continent and nestling its head in a crevice under the earth. So immense was Ba-Hui that its slightest stirring would shake the planet's foundations, causing the ground to seize and earth's mountainous veins to crumble, so it usually kept still. For this reason, Nanyu's people revered the deep mountain caves, and they made these sacred sites their places of ritual and sacrifice. In order to achieve closeness with their god, the people built their homes within these mountain caves and held elaborate sacrifices in the networks of caverns. The closer one came to Ba-Hui, the easier one might receive the god's favor. Their priests ruled over even the emperor, and the high priest — the source of the empire's authority — oversaw only the most magnificent sacrificial ceremonies.

Objectively speaking, there was nothing too shocking about Zhang's records of old Nanyu, excluding what was obviously fantasy. It was Zhang's crazed style and excessively alien citations that clashed with orthodoxy. His work had done little to earn academic recognition. Although I had been his friend for over a decade, I had to admit his hypothesis seemed like nothing but wishful thinking: having made a small discovery, he had become obsessed, seeking out evidence that confirmed his theories and disregarding the fundamental principles of archaeology. The vice president of the Sichuan Archaeology Institute, Professor Ke Jianhua, felt the same. He rejected Zhang's proposal to investigate the countryside, and instead sent him on a compulsory sabbatical; allegedly, this was for Zhang's health and peace of mind, to spend some time away from the cage of academia; effectively, to avoid any further negative repercussions for the institute. Of course, Zhang paid no heed to the words of the vice president. As I understood it, he took off for southwestern Sichuan on the second day of his vacation, April 2, survey tools in hand and luggage in tow, to commence the institute's first extralegal excavation.

The details of this round of research remain a mystery, but he and I made contact when he returned to Chengdu. On May 4, during an interview at the University of Sichuan, I received an unexpected phone call. He told me breathlessly that he had brought back an alarming discovery. I made haste to Beimen Station to receive him.

At first glance he was barely recognizable; his clothes were filthy and he wore a tattered trench coat with a bulging canvas backpack hauled over his shoulder. His shaggy hair framed a face flecked with stubble, and his left hand was loosely bandaged with blackened gauze. When he finally saw me, his tired eyes lit up and he embraced me briskly, already tripping over himself to tell me of the investigation's resounding success. He had discovered something that archaeology could not even imagine, he said: something that could capsize history as we knew it.

I remember that he spoke at great length in his excitement but somehow failed to divulge any substantial information. The sly devil avoided revealing any of his precious secrets, only repeating what an immense, important discovery he had made. I understood that he wished to protect his discovery until he could disclose it to the public, so I didn't press the matter. I remember asking him about the bandage on his hand. He told me he had sliced it after falling over a large pottery jar. He extracted a few pot shards from his canvas bag for me to study, saying he had kept the broken pieces.

I could easily perceive the pottery's exquisite crafts-manship. Traces of paint were discernible on the larger fragments. The meticulously drawn scales, in veinlike pattern, depicted a portion of a serpentine animal with violent realism. If these fragments were as ancient as Zhang claimed, then this piece was an equal — perhaps a usurper — of the masterpiece at Altamira. The pottery was curved slightly, making it trickier than a flat surface to grasp, and far trickier to paint upon. Yet the artisan had ingeniously exploited the natural contours of the material — the pottery, and the snake thereon, twisted as one. However, during my study of the fragment, I was compelled to an emotion I could not name. Distraught, anxious thoughts bubbled to the surface of my mind. I eventually noticed that the pottery shard leached a noisome ichthyoid scent, which I instinctively loathed. Zhang was more than familiar with the smell — he told me the odor had been left by a liquid stored in the large pot, which had spilled its contents all over his body when he stumbled over it. He guessed that it was some kind of fermented alcohol or herbal medicine. I doubted it was either.

I saw him home, and we began to discuss other things, though my heart honestly wasn't in it. I couldn't fathom why I felt so preoccupied, but the ancient, grotesque fish-smell of the pottery shard had evinced in me an indescribable reaction. Somehow, even after Zhang had returned the fragment to its burlap sack, the feeling persisted, and I fancied I could still smell the damned thing — weakly, yes, but maddeningly, imperceptibly definite. What's more, I saw hidden in Zhang's every gesticulation a compulsive, crazed excitement — though not too unusual, I supposed, in light of his recent discovery.

I could not have foreseen that we had just met for the last time. I concluded my visit to Sichuan University and returned to Hangzhou three days later. Another seven days thereafter, I gave Zhang a call to check in on his work. As any archaeologist would tell you, the idea of an undiscovered prehistoric civilization held an irresistible magic. To my surprise, his wife Wangyun answered the phone, grieving, and informed me that Zhang had been admitted to a mental hospital four days prior, for mania and severe neurosis. She said Zhang had been acting especially impatient since returning from his trip. He had taken to working nonstop in his study room, resting intermittently; he slept in his chair for two hours a night at most. He had forbidden anyone from touching his materials — in one of Zhang's rare episodes of rest, Wangyun had snuck into his study to tidy his desk, but he awoke immediately and became furious with her. After that, no one was even allowed near his study room. Following a ferocious argument, Wangyun left for her parents' home in a huff and did not speak with him after that. Then, on the midnight of May 10, her phone rang. Her neighbor had called to say her house had caught fire. Wangyun, rushing home, discovered that Zhang had tossed his neatly taken notes and research materials together in a metal bin and set them on fire. But he'd done it right next to the wastebasket, which also caught flame, and the whole study room soon followed. Miraculously, some bystanders noticed the smoke in time to stop the blaze from spreading, and in the end Zhang suffered only minor shock with no serious injuries. The neighbors suggested that Wangyun should see Zhang to the emergency room. Two days later, he was transferred to Chengdu Humane Mental Hospital.

Careful readers may already have some idea of what happened next. On the afternoon of May 24, Zhang took advantage of his ward's lunch break, stole an unattended doctor's coat, and slipped right out the front door of the mental hospital. Nonviolent patients who had made no previous escape attempts did not need to be kept under a nurse's supervision in the high-security ward. As far as the hospital was concerned, Zhang's breakout had been a "totally unpredictable accident." An investigation by the staff found that he had not stolen anything from the hospital, nor had he retrieved the personal items he had been admitted with, likely out of fear of alerting the hospital staff. He had, however, taken a personal journal, which he had previously applied to keep.

# PART TWO
# The Second Study of Western Sichuan

I have so far related Zhang's story in such detail so as to offer the reader some background on the one they are about to read. Above, I wrote that his disappearance sparked a discussion among academic circles, from which I readily excused myself. As his friend of over a decade, I would be caught dead before making a rash comment on his behavior; but, on the other hand, his proposals were nothing if not deviant. Even though I had finally caught a glimpse of that inscrutable pottery shard, I found it hard to purge my heart's innermost doubts and join the ranks of his defense. Fortunately, I didn't waste much thought on the matter. Zhang had disappeared quite completely, and although his family kicked up a swarm of resourceful, nosy journalists, their efforts earned them not a single lead. Since he had destroyed all of his records in the house-fire before his dispatch to the mental hospital, no one had any idea what his research had uncovered. As time inevitably passed, fervent discussion died down, and the story became just another unsolved mystery, a curiosity to be remarked upon over afternoon tea.

But something came up only a month and a half later. On the twelfth of July, I received an email from a mutual friend of Zhang's and mine, Dr. Yang Ye from the geology department of Southwest Jiaotong University. He had attached a few photocopies of something he said he had accidentally discovered while offering his condolences to Zhang's family: a fire-scorched notebook, from which he had salvaged a few pages of content. After getting a clear look at them, a wave of ecstasy overcame me — the dates, names, and addresses indicated that this was his travel notebook! He had neatly written out every location he had investigated — meaning that I could personally corroborate his discoveries and decrypt this enigma once and for all! Dr. Yang and a few of his friends, he said, were sifting through the locations one by one, searching for clues leading to Zhang's alarming discoveries. Remembering his injured left hand, I told them he had damaged it in a place where he had made a stunning discovery, as they might have been able to use that to sift through the information for that site.

My new information accelerated their search, allowing them to pinpoint the location of Zhang's research site: a village in Ya'an Prefecture, Shimian County,[15] near Chestnut Plains, known as "Lao Wa-lin" — and yet we consulted every level of administrative records for some mention of "Lao Wa-lin" to no avail. So Dr. Ye himself made the long trip south to Chestnut Plains, to ask some locals about the history of Lao Wa-lin. As it turned out, the name referred to an isolated region set in the deep mountains, accessible only via an arduous drive up a road scarcely wide enough for a small vehicle. The government had changed Lao Wa-lin's name to Xiayan[16] Village in the early 1890s to comply with subdivision laws, which explained why we had been unable to find it in any digital records.

Having learned this, I borrowed some vacation time to fly to Chengdu to prepare with the others for the investigation we had agreed to undertake. All told there were five of us on this excursion: Dr. Yao Zhenhua of the Sichuan University department of archaeology; Zhou Ziyuan, research associate of the Beijing Academy of Social Sciences; research associate Li Guohao of the Sichuan Cultural Anthropology Institute; Dr. Yang Ye,

15   As well as being the name of a remote county, Shimian also means "asbestos."

16   "Xiayan" literally means "beneath the cave."

a civil engineer from Southwest Jiaotong University; and I. Since we had no idea what we might run into, we decided to make our first trip a triage rather than a deep search. We would bring minimal sets of climbing gear, basic necessities, and some photographic equipment. We did whatever we could to keep the operation small-scale, and somehow managed to fit all of it, and ourselves, in the cars of Yang Ye and Yao Zhenhua.

The morning of July 22, we made it out to Chengdu, bearing toward Shimian County and arriving later that evening. We gathered a few more supplies and stopped to rest for the night. Early the next morning, we bid farewell to the roiling waves of the Dadu River to follow its tributary the Nanya upstream to the southern country, where it carved through the ascending hills all the way to Chestnut Plains. My memory of that part of the trip has already faded to a haze — I can recall only the dull fog that choked the skies, the pallid sunlight that trudged through the unbroken, undulating mountain range; and those few furtive glimpses I could catch of sunlight glinting weakly off the Nanya as it ran by the highway. At first we saw only crude thatch huts for local night watchmen, but soon we noticed homes of pitch-black wood in the old style seemingly placed at random. We passed a few as tall as three stories, steeped in untold history. The houses steadily grew larger, wider, and more frequent, until they seemed to merge together at the walls; we drove on as two dark hedges of chaotic edifice rose up and surrounded the road. We made it to Chestnut Plains by noon, feeling loath to stop the vehicle. We asked a few of the locals for directions and quickly located a guide willing to bring us to Xiayan. We ate a few simple things, then by our guide's suggestion left by the village's west side on a disused mountain road, toward a mountain range so massive it scraped the very skies.

We soon left the noise of the village behind us, driving ever deeper in. At last, we submerged into a silence knowable only in the wilderness. The roadside vegetation became lush and murky, higher and thicker in layers until it resembled the walls of an immeasurable labyrinth, enclosing us within. The wheels struck the potholes on the rugged little mountain road. Something in the grappling leaves and twigs seemed alive, beckoning, guiding us on our wandering way to an unknown world. Over the shadowed viridian maze towered a mountain range of majestic peaks and precipitous cliffs. In the distance, on the exposed ash-grey granite of those high cliffs, the jungled gleam of shrubs reticulating like scales gave us the striking impression of some gargantuan beast, the likes of which we had not yet begun to understand.

Even this wild realm, so isolated from civilization, did little to calm our spirits. On the contrary, we took to brooding on our own existence, small and frail as it was; we hoped against hope to glimpse some familiar trace of human activity — and thereby, some small vestige of comfort. To think we would descend even further into this savage abyss made one's already-repressed thoughts grow yet darker. Fortunately, as dusk had just begun to fall, we spied some mark of civilization at last, and the terror quickly fled. We first caught sight of some reclaimed land by the roadside, then spied some of the Yi tribe's ornaments hanging from the trees. Layered stone gradually became terraced fields. As the road twisted around a prominent hillside, a plain and simple Yi village cropped up out of nowhere. We quickly realized it was Xiayan — indeed, the Lao Wa-lin straight from the diary of Zhang Cunmeng! We had already arrived.

The ash-grey stonework and narrow, meagre windows silently told the village's ancient history. A few of the larger, more ancient wooden constructions had been eroded by winds and rain to possess a dark dendritic gloom. The majority of the village were old people and children dressed in the traditional attire of the Yi. Young adults in their prime, all seeking more gainful employment in the city, had left the area, smothering it in a desperate, decaying desolation. A crowd had already formed as our car pulled into the village; as the place seldom received outside visitors, we made for an attractive diversion. For us, this was a blessing, as the moment we brought out a picture of Zhang and asked after his whereabouts, many people recognized the photograph in our hands. They told us we should seek a man named E'li.

This E'li they spoke of was a sturdy middle-aged man with a healthy tan and a warm smile, whose Mandarin had been blended with the West Sichuan Yi dialect. He said he used to be a hunter, until Chestnut Plains had been designated a protected area. At that point, he started anew as a forest warden, and his decades of experience in the mountain forest had earned him peerless knowledge of the encircling territory. He easily remembered Zhang Cunmeng when we explained our visit, since the village rarely entertained company. Zhang had indeed spent four or five nights in the village, he said, relentlessly researching the local folktales and, what's more, surveying the surrounding terrain. E'li also said he had been puzzled by some of the other things Zhang had gotten up to, like offering him money to show him the way to a site called the "Erzi Cave."

Around those parts, the Erzi Cave was known as a cursed place. For generations, villagers had been taught to avoid the cave, although according to E'li no one knew exactly why. Some said the Erzi Cave was a bottomless pit reaching all the way down to hell. Some said it was a torturous cyclopean labyrinth that crushed all who were rash enough to enter. Still more said it was home to an enormously dangerous monster that none could meet and live to tell the tale. When he was a child, E'li did not believe in fairy tales, and he had once set out deep into the Erzi Cave by torchlight to finally get to the bottom of the question. He picked his way down the cavern until his torch flickered, and yet he still had not found its end, much less any beasts or monsters — however, something in that subterranean dusk summoned in him an unspeakable terror. Crushed between fear and darkness, he cut short his descent and made good his escape, never again to return.

How Zhang Cunmeng had learned of the Erzi Cave, E'li did not know. He had shown Zhang to the cave despite grave misgivings, although E'li had refused to enter with him (for reasons unknown even to himself), choosing merely to wait at the entrance. Zhang, having not made any special preparations, had entered the cave with what simple equipment he had. E'li remembered Zhang spending a great deal of time in the cave before eventually staggering out, battered and disheveled, a deep wound in his right hand, and his clothes stained with an odd substance from which diffused an ancient, unspeakably alien scent. Zhang, however, had told E'li with visible excitement that the wound (which he had seemed to completely disregard) was but a scratch compared to the discoveries he had made inside the cave.

This news powerfully excited us. It was indeed here where Zhang had received his injury, and, going by E'li's retelling, this Erzi Cave was quite possibly the place where Zhang had made his most important discovery. Three times we entreated E'li to take us there before he begrudgingly relented. We unloaded the camping and spelunking gear from the car and spent the evening in Xiayan Village.

The next morning we set off from Xiayan; under the guide of E'li we headed west along the path Zhang had taken into the heart of those nighted and desolate mountains. We made our way ahead through the low points of the mountain valleys, so as to carry our heavy equipment along what little path there was between the stunted trees and bushes. Occasional patches of bare earth eroded by centuries of roaming herds and piles of rock left behind as ancient indicators revealed, in rare glimpses, that this place had once been hunting grounds to the ancient Yi.

The path inexorably steepened. On all sides the terrain rose, or dropped, with lethal inclination, resembling even more than yesterday an impenetrable fortress. Deep granite cliffs flung themselves from cloud-piercing peaks in all directions; our mood was desolate. As the earth rose, the trees thinned and eventually succumbed to short mountain shrubs, for all the good it did our line of sight — those soaring peaks obscured our vision wherever we looked. The hermetic blockade permitted only a palm-sized patch of sky through its barrier. The mountains to the west grew larger, and white clouds hovered halfway up the snow-covered range — from a distance it was difficult to perceive where one ended and the other began. Faced with such mountains, any human could readily hallucinate a mysterious world, unknown to mankind, hidden within them. The strength of man, and even our modern civilization, was dwarfed in comparison to that savage majesty. We began to understand why the ancient Yi, living among that presence, had worshipped and made sacrifice to it as a god.

Near noon we reached what E'li had called the Erzi Cave. It sat at the foot of a precipitous cliff, at the bottom of a valley formed by prehistoric glaciers. The titanic mouth of the cave consisted of bare glacially carved rock covered in a thin layer of mud. Small mountain bushes grew overhead. Yang Hua, our geologist, inspected the cave entrance and the surrounding mountain topography, developing a preliminary theory — as he understood it, we were linked to the depths of the earth by an enormous fissure system whose cracks had been shaped by geological formations. At the end of the Ice Age, the glaciers had melted into the valley and poured into the cracks in the terrain. With the patience of eternity, the underground river had steadily eroded the rock around and within the cracks, until it formed the cavern system whose entrance we beheld. Some eons later, the glaciers had vanished, the underground river was dry, and the entire cave system lay completely exposed.

Although we had gotten along quite well with E'li up to this point, he swiftly and firmly refused our invitation to explore the cave together — though frankly, we were not surprised. Myths and taboos passed down through the generations had left a deep impression in his mind. He said he disbelieved the rumors about the Erzi Cave — and was convinced that there was nothing below — and yet each time he mentioned the place we clearly sensed, as before, the off-kilter manner of his speech. We therefore agreed that no matter what we found within, we would return within four hours. Further plans would be made from there. So resolved, our five-man team prepared our bags and spelunking essentials, and entered the deep, dark cave.

To this day, even despite our photographic evidence, I am uncertain whether that journey below was anything but a bizarre, grotesque night-terror. Though I still recall the innumerable, miraculous atrocities revealed to us; the abnormal, appalling process of our exploration; even the maddening misfortunes that befell me — all of this, in my memory, seems singularly unreal. Worse, the memories have been muddled with a certain set of disgusting legends I once read, and I am unable to distinguish what is speculation based on real events and what are wild imaginings spawned from those repulsive tales. The gloomy, mysterious atmosphere of the cave obviously exerted a subtle and peculiar influence on our minds, and we could not help but explain our horrifying discoveries — and the ancient, irreconcilably alien things who once lived here — with our most sinful and terrifying thoughts.

With carbide lamps held aloft in the cave's darkness, we followed the trail for a long time. The cave plunged far downward, far beyond our reckoning. As the path sloped ever deeper, its torturous lineament underwent vast changes, yet no matter how it contoured it remained remarkably wide throughout, never narrowing in the slightest. The cave swiveled in every kind of twist and bending slalom, but it always descended at roughly twenty to twenty-five degrees, seemingly stretching to bowels of the earth that humans had scarcely touched. There were few stalactites and stalagmites growing within, possibly due to our height above sea level and a temperature unsuitable for sedimentary formations. More often we encountered large pieces of gravel or flat rock surfaces smoothed over by passing water. In the acetylene blaze, these features spawned erratic shadows, elongating out from the flickering light that cast a foreboding pall over a cave already otherworldly. We did not encounter any byways worth mentioning on our journey, save a few cracks that had expanded across the surface of the cave wall. Most of them were only wide enough to reach a hand within, but a small number could accommodate one's body, squeezed in sideways. We stopped by those larger fractures to conduct some simple studies. We estimated their age to be much younger than the cave itself, likely torn open by geological effects after its formation. These traces of nature's horrifying power gripped us with an indescribable fear, as though gods lurking beneath the thick soil had torn scars into these walls in a display of tyrannical power. On the other hand, we found signs likely left by Zhang Cunmeng: arrows smeared with paint on the walls and glowsticks stuck in the crevices of what had been his last journey. The sight filled us with emotion. We knew by the markings that we were on the right track, but we could not resist poignant reminiscence over Zhang, who had disappeared from our safe and civilized world.

Our first surprise was abrupt. An hour had passed since entering the cave when we suddenly beheld a flat horizontal tunnel. It bore straight and level with an extremely regular circular outline, making it difficult to believably attribute to natural forces. Even by the ample light of our carbide lamps, we could only vaguely glimpse the tunnel's roof — and again we could find sedimentary formations on neither the floor nor the cavern ceiling. The gravel and pebbles scattered across other areas had also vanished completely.

This was not even the extent of our surprise. As we advanced slowly through this strange tunnel, we suddenly noticed colorful pictures painted on the cave walls. After a moment of shock we realized these were the remains of the "Ancient Country of Nanyu" mentioned by Zhang, and immediately we focused our attention on them. The two miraculous murals were about ten feet high by fifty or sixty feet wide, undoubtedly the work of several artists employed together. Subtle differences between scenes confirmed this theory, although it was challenging to conceive of how an ancient people had created such a magnificent work so far underground thousands of years ago.

The artwork contained a variety of scenes and told many stories, fluidly shifting from one scene to the next to form a seamless whole. The scenes progressed chronologically from the outside in, evidently for narrative purposes. Walking in the direction of the deeper caves, it was intuitive that the story illustrated the passage of time. With their simple composition and realistic structure, the murals shared a descriptive style with other famous prehistoric creations. Despite their simplicity, the beings on the wall moved vividly and the scenes were gravid with a tension evident in each highly technical brushstroke: this was definitely the work of observatory artists. We were able to decrypt their content after a holistic review and some cursory discussion. They told the story of a tribe who had discovered this cave, accepted to worship some kind of deity, then settled down and multiplied. Naturally the story incorporated some mythology, but something about this occulted, antediluvian civilization confounded and unsettled us.

According to the content of the paintings, the Ancient Country of Nanyu had once suffered a battery of cruel wars. Two tribes dressed separately in white and brown were locked in an overwhelming conflict; the white tribe were desperately outnumbered. Armed with crude spears and sticks, the brown tribe encircled and killed many of the white tribe's men. The remaining whites fled one after another toward the even more dangerous mountain range. Still the brown tribe pursued them, determined to eradicate what remained of the whites. The white tribe was driven to some low-lying ground between the mountain peaks — judging by the landmarks, the very valley that was home to the Erzi Cave. In those days, it seemed, there had still been a meandering river flowing into it. The hunters from the brown tribe climbed round the peaks surrounding the valley, embattling their enemies on all sides, ready to wipe them out. Then a figure painted in sheer white stood by the mouth of the cave and pointed a finger within. He appeared to call upon the near-defeated white tribe to follow him inside. In contrast to the rest of the figures, which were depicted coarsely and lacking distinguishing features, the man by the cave was drawn extremely finely. He wore a peculiar headdress and bore decorative designs on his body. On his hands and feet he wore furs from many animals, suggesting great import.

The story moved underground, and the man in the headdress led the survivors of the white tribe within. At all times, a shadowy bulk of scales lurked at the edge of their vision, some kind of immense reptilian creature imperceptibly advancing along with them. Suddenly, the leader lost his footing and fell into the river. The tribe watched helplessly by the shore as the current swept him further away, and he disappeared behind its gently winding corners. He was carried to a rapidly flowing narrow gully, plunged down a waterfall into a deep pool, and surfaced upon a flat riverbank.

A grotesque group of reptiles — with long, slender humanoid torsos and flat serpentine heads, depicted in green and grey paint — happened upon him. Where human arms should have been, they instead possessed thin forelimbs covered in unmistakably ophidian scales. They lacked hindlegs as well, and stood upright on elongated, coarse trunks, like a snake. They gathered around the body of the man with the headdress, gesturing as though in discussion. Nearby lay an enormous snake — gigantic beyond imagination — resting inside a pile of boulders. The painters had left the silhouette of this beast unfinished, coloring only the inconceivable flat head, much larger than a person, and a portion of the body. Meanwhile it looked as if the unnatural creatures had reached a consensus; they lifted the man into the mouth of the giant snake, which swallowed him. The creatures circled around the snake's head and prostrated themselves before it, seemingly carrying out an arcane ritual.

The subsequent scenes were the mural's most impenetrable. Once again the giant snake opened its enormous maw; and within stood a new serpentiform creature, but this one was different from the others. It was painted in white; it wore the tribe leader's headdress and furs, and it bore the same ornamental designs on its slender body. The white creature began to lead the other green-grey things away from the giant snake, to seek the remaining members of the white tribe. The humans also prostrated themselves before the snake-things, expressing their respect and fear, receiving the monsters as honored guests. Finally, the dull-green snake-things led the white tribe out of the cave, beseeching the incomprehensible, many-scaled monster to swallow the brown tribe whole, exterminating the white tribe's enemy.

Our group of five entertained no small discussion of the meaning hidden in the murals. The most sensible explanation was put forward by Zhou Ziyuan, who was well acquainted with mythology. He believed the content depicted in these scenes was an exact confirmation of how heroic mythology was elaborated on within modern theory. From the perspective of comparative mythology, the mural described the adventures of the hero in the headdress. He led his people into the cave because of the war, which symbolized that he had been summoned to embark on a journey. Falling into the river represented the danger and suffering of his experience, while rescue by the snake-like creatures meant he had received outside help. Entering the snake's mouth symbolized the trials of the hero, while the appearance of the white snake-like creature represented the sublimation of the hero after passing through the trials. Finally, leading the snake-creatures to obliterate the enemy tribe symbolized the return of the hero.

This theory explained why the white snake-creature had worn the same headdress and furs, and was depicted with the same decorative pattern; this strange animal was the man who had been offered into the snake's mouth. Entering the mouth meant death; this was a metaphor for the elimination of the hero's secular identity. That which was reborn within the mouth of the snake was a being higher than the material world — a god, or something approaching one. Replacing the original image of the man with the image of a serpentine figure was merely the visualization of this process. Naturally, the hero was still a human being; the mural merely utilized the expressive technique of symbols. Many primitive religions depicted priests or wizards as creatures different from ordinary people, even directly elevating them as the heirs of the gods. This symbol may have originated from the priests imitating these sacred snake-like creatures by wearing snakeskin (or the skin of another type of reptile) during sacrifices, just like a shaman covering himself in furs or an American Indian wearing feathers.

We could not reach a consensus on whether or not the serpent-creatures actually existed, if only because Yao Zhenhua — always the most radical in his speculation — thought they really may have depicted a type of long-extinct reptilian hominid. The rest of us suspected they were only the imaginings of primitive humans. Although, considering the images of half-human, half-snake creatures in China's own ancient legends, this was not an utter impossibility.

Even so, we did not linger for long. After careful photography of the entire mural, we lifted our carbide lamps and proceeded down the tunnel, hoping for more ancient artefacts to advance our understanding of Zhang's revelations. Yet as we emerged from the other end of the tunnel, what our eyes beheld shocked us speechless.

The passage emptied out into an immeasurably gigantic hole. When we turned our high-strength torches — which we had specially brought to illuminate the far ends of such crevasses — to maximum brightness, the effort was useless. Apart from the stone walls surrounding the aperture, our torches revealed nothing but dense shadow in every direction, as if we had departed the cave for a lightless oblivion. Some time passed before it dawned on us that this was an unimaginably large shaft. Even Yang Hua, who had spent his life in the geology department, was unable to explain how such a cyclopean shaft could have formed.

A path extended from the portal's right edge, scarcely wide enough for three men to walk abreast. It clung tightly to the wall of stone, sinking gently into the shaft's far depths. Its surface was decked with irregular potholes, chipped stones, and smooth rocks; and the trail was of constant width throughout. The stone wall revealed cutting marks upon inspection. This proved man had carved the passageway, although it was unfathomable how those primitive Stone Age denizens had accomplished this feat. All the chisel marks had been eroded to exceptional smoothness over time — indeed the result of generations of people leaning against the rock face as they descended. Our curiosity was piqued. What lay below that was worthy of the ancestors accomplishing this work and walking this trail year after year?

We could not resist. In single file and clinging to the stone wall, we made our way to the deeper regions of the shaft. Quickly we were pleased to find the walls of the passageway were also covered in many more murals. The maturity of the paint remnants and the degeneration of the surface informed us these murals dated not to the same period, but were in fact becoming far more ancient as we trod further away from the tunnel. In contrast to the large-scale murals, these were smaller — most only a few square feet in size — and possessing a more casual style; some multi-colored, others simple outlines sketched in white. Some displayed a single scene; others were a combination of multiple ones. Some were simple narratives; others were difficult to understand — probably incorporating elements of religious significance from legend. All the same, no two were alike, and there was no scheme of fixed patterns and symbols. Perhaps the purpose of these murals was not mere decoration; perhaps they served as a record of important events, preserving cultural heritage. We investigated and recorded as much as we could from each mural we saw, despite limited time — and with each new inspection, fear and doubt gripped our hearts ever tighter. Those first people who had once walked here, like a river that dripped into the sea of life, bore no resemblance whatsoever to anything we had seen before. Only an infinite strangeness still survived them, leaving us uncertain whether we could even dare to term those people as human.

These were clearly the descendants of the white tribe from the tunnel murals, and this deep cave their sacred ground and holy temple. Certain murals, mythological in nature, depicted the gods they worshipped — an incomparably giant snake and those serpentiform creatures with the slender forelimbs who meandered forward on their thick coarse tails. The murals told us those peculiar creatures were the progeny of the divine snake; its messengers. In the lowest depths of the sacred cave they lived in a great glorious city, with all manner of edifices towering therein. Between these structures grew an odd garden of huge mushrooms, around the outline of a queer open square that followed no rules — Babylon paled in comparison to its marvelous majesty. Yet below that fabulous city lay an even larger world full of rolling hills, steep valleys, vast plains, and deep oceans. It was there that the divine snake, large as a mountain, swam and took its rest.

Just like in the murals from the tunnel, those grotesque serpent-things were again used to depict the high-caste priests and persons of interest living in the Ancient Country of Nanyu. In a series of narrative murals, the creatures conducted rituals, led the army, and imparted technical skills to mankind. Far fewer creatures appeared here than in the mythical city, and they had been rendered in richer detail — like the humans, they wore strange ornaments or wrapped themselves in animal pelts. These decorations convinced us that the serpent-men were merely an expressive technique to mark the social status of different tribespeople. Besides those symbolic creatures, the murals contained many other varieties of monster, seemingly degenerate or dissimilated humans, whose appearance inspired a terror previously unique to nightmares. These things were not even exceptional; in fact, there were three types of different exotic beast that commonly appeared in the murals.

One was a giant ape similar to a human, tall as one and a half or two men — physically strong, with forearms hanging to the knees, and the ability to walk upright like a gorilla. Their smooth hairless bodies, flat head shape, and flatter faces imbued these creatures with even more human-like features. These animals seemed to be beasts of burden for the ancients of Nanyu, carrying heavy loads on their backs or scaling cliffs in many of the murals.

The second kind of animal was more disgusting: like savage humans who had devolved into beasts. Their hairless bodies were of similar proportion to a human's, but bowed at the waist. Like a dog or a bear, they used their four limbs to run at high speeds, hunting prey and pursuing the enemies of the ancients of Nanyu. We discovered in some more detailed murals that their forepaws did not have short toes like canids and ursids use for running, but long ones like a primate's ... or a human's. They had slender splaying knuckles, four fingers that bent in either direction, and a grasping thumb. From the tip of each slender finger grew a sharp talon-like nail long enough to rend flesh — it was so similar to both a human's palm and a wild animal's claw that we were left with a peculiar sense of unease. And yet the true horror was still the animal's face: more man-like than any ape, but there was something it ... lacked. We refused to call it man; it was a mélange of human and animal. Its forehead and its eyes were human, save its missing eyebrows and hairless scalp; but the collapsed nose-bridge, its upturned nostrils, its protruding jaw, and its formidable incisors and canines belonged to a hideous, violent beast. All throughout, the beasts maintained a crazed, monstrous face, devoid of any expression that man ought to exhibit. We were uncertain whether to feel fortunate or fearful.

The final beast, the shortest of the three, looked like a bald monkey or an unnatural dwarf, with outgrown forearms and stubby hindlegs. Upright, they were about half the height of a human; but their distinguishing feature was their head, which was far too large for their bodies — more or less the same size as an adult human's, except with a pair of incommensurately huge eyes and exaggerated ears. They seemed to be scouts for the ancients of Nanyu; they scaled trees with their slender arms to spot distant quarries.

There was no agreement among us whether these bizarre images — and those of the snake-priests — were symbolic expressions of social class, or whether such unnatural creatures had once existed in reality. At least, we reached no definite conclusion while studying the murals. Nonetheless we hoped with our whole hearts these were merely images employed by prehistoric painters, and simply difficult for modern humans to intuit. We were already discomfited by the idea that those beasts, which may or may not have been human, had potentially possessed the intelligence to cooperate with humans on complex tasks. If true, it was the substance of nightmares.

The murals showed relatively fewer normal humans in comparison to the number of these weird animals. The ones we could see were always conducting activities in the temple or the cave nearby. The humans were divided into two separate classes: a small portion served as craftsmen or servants, doing menial labor, preparing the food, cleaning the temple, and painting murals. The larger portion was provided for, like aristocracy, and scarcely needed to work at all. The murals exhaustively illustrated their obesity, with some of them so bloated they could not even stand — as though this matter were both necessary and important to flaunt. The structure of their society greatly surprised us, since we had never before seen a primitive civilization that could tolerate such a high proportion of non-working people. Moreover, all of the people represented were young adults: we could almost find no other age group of human beings — the murals contained nothing about childbirth, childrearing, aging, or funeral rites.

We also found reason to believe this cave was not their only homestead. Several murals exhibited the vast size of the Ancient Country of Nanyu. A group of people led every kind of strange animal out of the cave to new frontiers, new settlements — typically, enormous and deep caverns. The ancients of Nanyu seemed to believe these caves were connected to the underground world where the divine snake lived, and were therefore sacred. The murals hardly mentioned what lay between these settlements. Each and every cave acted as an independent tribe, or city, scattered amidst the mountains of south-western Sichuan.

Some of the other murals displayed wars between the Ancient Country of Nanyu and other tribes and countries. The later murals depicted scenes of several settlements at once invading, or being invaded by, another kingdom; yet, these wars were waged not for territory ... but food. Those humanoid beasts would storm the other villages in packs, murdering any living thing they could find. They would cunningly ambush armies trying to cross the steep mountains, breaking up any groups of soldiers too slow to react, or simply pushing them down the mountain. The half-ape giants would lumber over the battlefield after the killings and bring the slain corpses back to the cave. We had known that cannibalism was not exactly unimaginable in the dawn of humanity, yet still we shuddered to think of such organized efforts to make prey of other people. Even more terrifying was the ancients' attitude toward predation, which was far different from the cannibalistic societies we were familiar with. The latter commonly attributed special religious or social significance to the practice — Aztecan blood sacrifice appeased the gods; New Guinean natives swallowed their old to reduce extraneous consumption of food. To these ancients, however, the people of other tribes were nothing but a daily food source, like an additional form of game animal. They held no grand ceremony for the slaughter of man, nor did they view human flesh with any precious significance other than as food. A strange fantasy took hold of us, suggesting that these ancestors were not, after all, human; rather, that they were wicked abominations in the form of men.

After another twenty minutes on that small passage-way, skeletal remains began to appear, scattered across the ground. Yao Zhenhua had considerable experience researching fossils; he informed us, from a glance at some of the easier specimens, these were ancient bones. As we descended, the skeletons multiplied, some of them still completely intact. Even now we knew not what we had discovered. The greater part of the bones had survived without any signs of trauma or animal tooth marks. Sometime later, approaching the terminus of the passageway, we witnessed something truly shocking.

It was the perfectly preserved skeleton of an unknown species, some large four-legged beast with a humanoid S-shaped spine. Its skull and other fine bones indicated a highly evolved primate or a human, but its prognathic jaws had the sharp incisors and giant canine teeth of a wild animal. We stopped to carry out a closer investi-gation — and realized, with growing revulsion, this was the very same hairless, beast-like human-creature we had seen in the murals. The emergence of this skeleton proved it: every hateful monster we had seen in those murals had once walked this majestic cave. I tremble merely to think of it.

This unexpected, looming horror was both sudden and short-lived. We picked our way around the skeleton, using our torches to navigate the bottom of the natural shaft — and were greeted by a maddening sight. Before us stretched an incredibly vast open plain, piled with behemoth platforms of stone. Throughout lay debris fallen from on high among a field of ash-grey bones. We had no way to guess how many had died here, nor what fate had befallen them. Some bones had been piled into small mounds, but most were scattered chaotically around. The dry underground environment had preserved much of their original appearance — the lonely scattered bones were perfectly intact, as if someone had nonchalantly left a body on the floor to decay for millennia. Human bones could be seen alongside the remains of the human-like quadrupeds, the half-ape giants, the small gibbon-things, and the skeletons of some unthinkable anthropoids with severe deformities. The majority of the bones had retained a natural posture without any serious damage. Whatever those ancient denizens had encountered, they had not resisted, or could not have resisted in time.

We acclimated to the deliriating scene, stumbling through the scattered bones and attempting to observe the other contents of the cave's depths, while going to great efforts not to imagine exactly what had happened here. This natural shaft originally had two exits other than the small ledge we had taken on the way down. One was a narrow crevice in the northwestern corner; the other was a large tunnel leading east. However, the latter had apparently suffered a grave landslide, leaving the entire thing impassable. On the floor between shattered rocks and white bones, one could find original tools from the era; stone-cut knives, broken pieces of pottery.... We had reason to believe that only the few artefacts that stood the test of time remained, and there had once been much more.

Luckily — or unluckily — the ancients, in their passion for artistry, had tessellated the cavern floor in cultural records. The murals here all depicted a common theme: sacrifice, loathsome sacrifice. Evidently this wide-open cave was once their sacrificial ground. Although the paintings lacked detail, our imaginations filled in the gaps and tinted the ominous festival in an even more sinister light. The ancients brought forth humans, and only humans, for their sacrificial offerings; however, the offerings were not captives from other tribes, but the fat, bloated aristocrats who never labored. In fact, according to the murals, these obese bodies were not the nobles of Ancient Nanyu, but livestock specially reared for offering to the gods. The scale of the depicted sacrifices was incomprehensible, which implied these ceremonies were none too frequent. What's worse — we began to suspect that, sooner or later, everyone in Ancient Nanyu was offered to the divine snake. This may have been why the murals contained so few older people — no one ever lived that long.

About a dozen priests — all portrayed as serpentiform creatures — and an ordinary human man, adorned in fabulous ornaments, conducted this great and terrible rite, lighting a massive bonfire at the bottom of the shaft. The younger tribespeople, not yet ripe for sacrifice, surrounded the pit and beat the ground. Those who had been chosen gathered in the center of the shaft, dancing an unnatural dance. One by one they climbed atop the high stone dais, where a four-legged hominid beast stood decorated in strange patterns. It knocked the sacrifices down and neatly bit open their flabby throats. Then two priests — again, painted as the ophidians — took hold of the corpse, disemboweled it with a sickening dagger, and cast it down from the platform. Next, the half-ape giants carried the body to the snake-priests assembled at the perimeter, who took it to the now-collapsed eastern tunnel — and we dared not speculate what became of them after that. At the height of the Ancient Country of Nanyu's most glorious period, this temple alone had seven stone daises simultaneously conducting ritual sacrifice.

Out of all the murals regarding sacrifice, we were most interested in one on the shaft's western stone wall. Compared to the others, this one looked as if it had been done in a hurry. Scrawled and disorderly, and without careful composition or use of color, it portrayed a sacrifice of unprecedented scale and chaos. All of the living creatures in the painting — whether human or terrifying hominid — had a crazed and distorted look on their faces. The ceremony was no longer confined to the surface of the high stone daises, and the sacrifices were no longer just the chosen people. In every corner of the cave, men with handheld blades, or the hominid monsters they drove forward, slaughtered not only the fattened people but also the still-unripe youths, and even the half-human beasts. The bodies piled in heaps; yet the slaughter showed no signs of slowing — and, most eerily, there were no ophidians to be seen. What could this mean? Did they lose the tradition of nominating priests over time and forget the process of making sacrifices? Or did they face an even more terrible situation, so much so that they resorted to these ghastly measures to entreat the gods for help? We had no answers to these questions, having endured too much doubt and fear already — we could only stagger among them, bearing inhuman terror and confusion, discovering one astonishing fact after another. We made some simple records of the bottom of the shaft, then left that dreadful place by the crest of rock in the northwest corner. Behind it extended a narrow and sinuous passage, followed by an inconceivably gargantuan cavern.

White bones stretched before us wherever we walked, but the bones in this cavern had changed. We now saw children's bones — ordinary children's bones. Most of the skeletons in these piles had belonged to infants, or toddlers of only a couple of years. A small number of adult remains, too, lay in the admixture. We examined these and discovered the majority had been women — seemingly suggesting this was a place for raising and protecting future generations. Paintings on the walls supported this hypothesis, illustrating a rare distinction between the sexes, with contents limited to themes of sexual intercourse, childbirth, and childrearing. This was doubly astonishing considering the earlier murals we had seen were remarkable in their entire absence of any depiction of family life. As we crept deeper into the cave, we lit the surroundings with our strong torches in an attempt to uncover anything that might help us understand these timeless, otherworldly ancestors; it was then that we discovered that mural — that answer to the mystery we had long cradled in our hearts, and the final piece of the puzzle that tore our minds in two.

The mural showed a ceremony, performed by several priests depicted as serpentine creatures. The participants included all of the images from the previous paintings: the half-human half-ape giants, the quadruped hominids, the gibbon-dwarves, and some ordinary people, along with many young infants, perhaps only recently weaned. During the ceremony the priests would inspect each child carefully, then paint one of six symbols on each of them, designating them into groups.

The first group of children drank a liquid from a spherical pot; then the half-human half-ape giants led them away. The second group of children drank a liquid from a long pot, then the four-legged humanoid beasts led them away. The third group of children drank a liquid from a huge jar, then the strange gibbon-like dwarves led them away. The fourth group of children, who were explicitly drawn as separate boys and girls, were returned to the childcare area to be taken care of by the women. The fifth group of children were chosen to be the sacrificial humans, and like the other sacrifices, they were to live a labor-free life. The sixth and smallest group were to be the raised by the ordinary humans, who performed simple menial tasks and drew the murals.

The mural then extended in all four directions, illustrating the different fates of these children in further detail. Each child would increasingly grow to resemble the group that had led them away.

The first group of children would become tall and strong and take care of the heavy work. The second group of children would crawl on the ground on their hands and feet, studying hunting with the four-legged humanoid beasts. The third group of children's eyes and ears would enlarge, and they would climb trees alongside those uncanny ancient midgets. The fourth group of children would become precocious, begin to fornicate, and bear even more ordinary children once they reached a certain age. The fifth and sixth groups of children would become utterly similar to those images of humans we had seen in the previous murals.

Once he understood the horrors that the murals implied, Zhou Ziyuan fell limply to the ground, his face pale. The others were shaken too, and could not help but lower themselves to the ground in an attempt to retain their composure. We briefly made eye contact. None opened their mouth to speak, but we all knew what the others were thinking. Could it be that those strange, hateful images we had seen in the murals, and those detestable, deformed bones scattered across the shaft-bottom, were human? The half-apes, the quadrupeds, and the gibbons — were they really the flesh and blood compatriots of those abominable ancestors? Was there actually a bizarre and occulted technique by which these ancestors transformed their descendants into inhuman deformities in order to maintain their grotesque and terrifying generational traditions?

After enduring such an eerie revelation, the others wished to return. They had lost the will to continue. Considering the horrifying iteration of revelations we had encountered, we doubted we would last the slightest additional shock. Furthermore, we had already burned more than half of our allotted time; we had to quickly depart this frightening place if we were to make it back on time and meet with E'li.

I, however, wished to continue exploring. Since entering the second cave, we had started to detect a faint and peculiar scent. The others attributed it to an air blockage, but I lucidly recalled this scent from my final meeting with Zhang Cunmeng. Both his clothes and that strange shard of broken pottery he had retrieved from here had been drenched in this weird odor. I carefully traced the source of the smell — it was emanating from the third cavern at the back of the cave. Thus, I suggested that the others stay and rest while I used this time to carry out a simply survey of the back of the cave alone. With their consent, I removed my luggage, brought a carbide lamp and a camera, and followed the faint smell into the cave.

I myself have no way to be sure of what exactly happened thereafter. For the longest time, I have tried to attribute that experience to over-exposure to horrifying truths, hallucinations conjured by a mind on the brink of collapse. After all, there is no evidence to corroborate my experience, and there were no witnesses to what I am about to describe. Some things, of course, were definitely real — like the cave's environment and arrangement, and ... that mural.

This chamber was far smaller than the other two caverns, about as big as a large hall; twenty feet at its highest point. Left of the entrance were several disorganized rows of ancient pottery covered in a thick layer of dust. The pots were about a foot high and decorated in a mosaic of scintillating patterns and adornments. Most of them were already broken, leaving only a pile of dust-covered shards, yet a few had survived in perfect condition, their openings sealed with muddy clay. I picked one up and shook it gently — it seemed to still hold some liquid. Another jar, apparently recently smashed, lay by the entrance — its internal surfaces lacked the thick layer of dust that blanketed the other relics, and its bottom still held the shallow dregs of a viscous black liquid. The peculiar stench that was smothering the entire chamber had billowed up from this black liquid. This was obviously the jar Zhang had accidentally broken during his inspection several months ago; its broken pieces had been carefully sorted into a small pile separate from the other pots. Next to the rows of pottery another passageway led upward; but it had already collapsed. Boulders had fallen into a high pile at the passageway's exit, leaving only a narrow gap to mark the original aperture. To its right was an especially complex painting.

It depicted a narrative like the ones we had seen elsewhere, though I dare not claim that I fully comprehended it. The mural portrayed yet another ceremony, comprised of several ophidian priests and an ordinary person in gorgeous adornments. I had seen this figure before in the sacrificial murals within the shaft — he seemed to be the conductor of the sacrifice. During the ceremony, the priests would open the man's chest with a weird stone dagger, then rub a black liquid into the wound. In the next scene, a reptilian creature burst forth from the man's stomach and clawed its way out. The priests would then flay the corpse of its skin, creating from it a kind of scroll covered in strange symbols. Undoubtedly, this was the mysterious leather scroll from the Cabot Archaeological Museum — the legendary *zi suo mo* — and yet, this scene confounded me. Was this atrocious serpent a genuine prehistoric organism, or did the ancients of Nanyu merely rely on this method to breed their sacred totem? Or was this nothing more than another symbolic artistic expression of the rituals necessary to attain priesthood?

I did not study it too deeply. After some simple photography, I continued to the lower levels of the cavern, seeking still more discoveries My carbide lamp illuminated an object that was not out of the ordinary, but nevertheless completely exceeded my expectations — a pile of dirty and tattered clothes stuffed behind a boulder. I advanced several steps and overturned the clothes, hoping for some information.

A torrent of fear and disgust washed over me. A mess of rotten hair and flesh lay swaddled in the rags, ripped and torn so severely it was impossible to distinguish the original face. I could merely determine that it had been a person — or something a person had left behind. There was not a single bone in the whole arrangement, only a thin layer of fetid flesh attached to the underskin, as though it had been brutally stripped from a human body. And yet there was no trace of blood on the ground, nor any other suspicious marks, almost as if it had been brought in from elsewhere. What thing had committed such handiwork? And more importantly — who had this been?

Suddenly, I heard the crushing sound of loose stones colliding nearby. I raised my carbide lamp and turned vigilantly to the source, and I froze in terror. The bright light revealed an appalling scene I will never be able to forget. The veil between reality and fantasy had lifted. The nightmares of my imagination appeared before me, snapping my already tightened nerves. A terror beyond my wildest fears drilled into me, and condensed into the freakish, maddening dreams that have plagued me every night ever since.

I beheld a towering serpentine beast, contorting its body as it slithered down from the mound of boulders. Its head was massive and flat, and speckled green-grey scales covered its smooth, slender body — just like in the murals. It groped its way across the rock heap with thin, scaly foreclaws. Emerging from the crevice behind it were two identical creatures, all making their way toward me. The near snake insinuated its way to the ground and raised itself like a viper, exposing its milky-white belly before twisting its tail and gliding closer. It raised a lean claw and, swallowing its forked purple tongue, pronounced a string of strange syllables in an empty, hollow voice. I wanted to flee, but I was fixed to the ground as though by some sorcery. Fear paralyzed my body, and I could not even close my eyes to escape the things I was seeing.

The ophidian creature came closer and closer; its claws nearly touched my body. Again I heard those unnatural syllables in that empty, hissing voice. Suddenly, I was aware of something, but my instincts were moving even faster. Before I could sort out the contents of my mind, unstoppable fear quenched my last thought, and I remembered nothing more. Fear broke the spell cast over me and I burst into screams. Holding my lamp aloft, I ran — almost rolled — to the door, tripped on a rock, staggered and hit the ground, and plunged into a merciful coma.

When I regained consciousness, I found the other members of the exploration team gathered around me. The snake-creatures and the pile of vile rotten flesh had vanished. I stuttered and stumbled through the previous events, but they did not believe me. They thought I had suffered a spontaneous traumatic nervous breakdown. Hearing my screams, Zhou Ziyuan had rushed into the cavern first. He thought he saw something crawl into the crevice above the boulders, but he dismissed it as the shifting torchlight shadows. Moreover, both he and Li Guohao had checked the crack — the collapsed stones had almost completely obstructed the ascending passage, leaving only enough space for a man to crawl through. It was hard to imagine that any large creature could pass in or out. They had, however, discovered a worn book not far from where they found me. It was a dirty green notebook, about the size of a hand, with many things scribbled inside.

And just like that, we concluded our frightening adventure and returned to the surface as planned.

That evening in Xiayan Village, we carefully studied the notebook we had retrieved. It was undoubtedly an artefact left by Zhang Cunmeng. Though the others found this surprising, I was extremely calm, calmer than I expected, when I heard the news. The notebook contained eccentric sketches of indecipherable intent: giant twisted buildings, convoluted patterns, and sculptures whose style we could not trace. This convinced us that Zhang Cunmeng had suffered complete and utter mental collapse. His ultimate whereabouts, and how this notebook appeared in that horrifying cave, were still a mystery — one I fear will never be solved. On the last page of the notebook, we found the following mess of text, written unsteadily as though by someone without fine control of their hand:

> This is the end. Again I dreamt of that city. I know it lies beneath, but the cave has no way in. I think I've broken several bones, but I am not in pain. I have no fear; it told me not to worry. I can finally enter; I am already a child of Ba-Hui. I believe it. I believe in Ba-Hui and

all of his other names ... the Great Dragon ...
Yig ... Kukulkan ... Father of Serpents. I will
shed my body and enter that great glorious
city. If anyone is reading this notebook —
don't come looking for me. Don't.

Reading these words, I began to shudder uncontrollably.
The others were so focused on the inexplicable text
that they failed to notice, but I knew. I knew the words
revealed an unnamable horror.

Because I remember the purple forked tongue of
that ophidian monster, issuing forth weird syllables in
a voice hollow and hissing. I remember, because it was
no brutal hiss. It was not even a mysterious and intricate
alien language. It was my name.

*The End*

O nce the Researcher had completed his narrative, my guests and I all waited in silence while I gathered my thoughts. Many would think that his story was a preposterous one, perhaps nothing more than the ravings of a disturbed and clinically insane mind or the concoction of an over-active imagination. I, however, knew differently. The Researcher had mentioned Yig and Kukulkan, fearsome serpentine deities, though neither held domain in this part of the world. The Plumed Serpent Kukulkan reigned over the steamy jungles of Mesoamerica, the cries of the human sacrifices to honor his name still resonant through the ages. Another abomination entirely was Yig, that shunned and feared father of serpents that haunts the American plains and whose followers rendered the nights hideous with the ceaseless beating of their tom-tom drums. Snake worship was not unknown in Asia; indeed, China was steeped in legends of dragons, though few realized that their myths of flying antediluvian wyrms had far more historical grounding than even the most unorthodox of paleontologists would expect. Whether Ba-Hui, Yig, Kukulkan, and other mythological snake gods were separate entities or in fact the same remnant of a primeval horror that could reawaken at any time, I would need to investigate further. If prehistoric civilizations remain secretly buried beneath the lonely mountains and dark caves where many a forgotten creature made its home, then they could cause unforeseen calamity in the future.

His story finished, the Researcher fell once more into complete silence. It was of no consequence: I had learned from him what I needed to know for the present. My thoughts now turned to the second of my guests. I had watched this man for many weeks, though always at a distance until the right opportunity had presented itself. Unlike my three other guests, this person was not of the academic inclination, and had it not been for a certain degree of talent in the art of painting would have been of entirely no consequence due to his habit of spending lengthy periods of time comatose under the influence of various narcotics and intoxicants. It was for this reason I had decided to name him the Dreamer.

From the box I now pulled out a framed picture of the most unimaginably beautiful landscape ever envisioned. Although it was not to my individual liking — myself far preferring landscapes of near-impenetrable darkness where formless voids gnaw shapeless and ravenous in the endless night — I could still appreciate the skill involved in its composition. The painting depicted a gorgeous natural landscape of breathtaking boundlessness, captured by a hand that transcended mortal skill. Green hills, sparkling rivers, billowing clouds seemed to almost leap out of the painting. A real Shangri-La.

"You say that you saw this landscape in a dream?" I asked the Dreamer. He was the most extroverted of my guests and was proud to have the chance to discuss his work.

"Not quite," he said. "I dreamt of the man who dreamt of this land. He was a painter and a dreamer just like me.

*He is the one who first created this painting; I merely copied what the dream revealed to me. In my visions I saw his story: how he came to be, how he came to create this painting, and where its creation led him."*

"And this painting I now hold?"

"*I composed it after awaking from my dream. I was afraid that I would forget my wonderful dream and so painted this immediately before I forgot. But a dream like that ... it was too vivid to be forgotten."*

*I considered the painting once more. It was indeed a work of great craft and inspiration, undoubtedly worth a fortune if it were to ever sell on the open market, though that was now an impossibility since it had fallen into my possession.*

"*Do you often dream of alien lands and other worlds?" I asked.*

*The Dreamer gave a soft sigh. "I often walk the Dream-lands that exist on the other side of our waking world. The strange and ancient cities outside space, the lovely unbelievable gardens across ethereal seas — all have lain before me during my nightly excursions."*

*Placing the picture back in the box lest its beauty distract me further, I nodded to the Dreamer to recount his tale of what he had seen beyond the wall of sleep.*

"*North of the city," he began, "there lay a black tower...."*

# Nadir

NORTH of the city there lay a black tower.

It was a stone tower of immense ill-omen, both ancient and tall, far exceeding any structure familiar to mankind, like those high mountains penetrating into unknown outer space toward which no man dared to venture. For the people of the city — no matter where they stood — every time they raised their heads to the northern skies, the tall tower would always be visibly protruding upward above the city's buildings, silhouetted against the sky with gloomy disdain for the world below.

Nobody seemed to know the history of this tower, and nobody wished to unearth its secrets. The legends surrounding the tower were incoherent, vague, and often with nightmarish qualities. Some believed it was a staircase leading to the Halls of the Gods, and the Heavenly Palace built atop the tower was surrounded by clouds throughout the year. Long, long ago, in the infancy of mankind, the gods would ride the moonlight to the peak of the tower and dance to all different styles of music. Other legends claimed that a group of beings completely unlike mankind had built the tower, with the aim of climbing up to the sky and overthrowing the gods' rule. However, the gods learned of their plot and destroyed their city, banishing them forever. Only the tower was left behind to serve as a warning to those who would dare to challenge the gods. However, there is a more recent story — though a story still much older than the city itself — that speaks of a man who once climbed the tower. In this story, a reckless and crazed fool attempted to ascend to the tower's peak and enter the realm of the gods. Yet nobody ever knew what he had seen, as when the fool returned, nobody could understand the absurdities he described.

Regardless of the truth of the matter, the tower was certainly extremely old; far older than the city itself. It had watched as wandering herdsmen led their woolen flocks across the shallow riverbanks. It had watched as prospectors excavated their first chunk of precious ore. It had watched masons build their first magnificent palace, and it had watched when priests sang their first hymn of divine praise. Every generation of the city came into the world, grew old, and passed away under its silent watch.

Once, there were some bold youths who dared to approach, or claimed to approach, the tower. Those who returned from the expedition told of a grey forest at the foot of the tower that had long since died, containing many large but incomplete blue-grey stone statues. Only a small number of these statues remained stubbornly standing; the majority lay fallen among the grey and black thorn bushes. The remaining features of these statues were grotesque and terrifying, as if in imitation of indescribably strange things, leaving little doubt as to what had led to their doom.

These stories exacerbated the peoples' revulsion of the tower, until gradually the inhabitants of the city began to subconsciously avoid all mention of it. They began to avoid the desolate lands north of the city. It was thus that the area became an enigma, spoken of only in legends and fireside stories. The people reached a common understanding. The best way to deal with the tower was to leave it alone until the slow passing of time brought about its collapse. Everyone believed that one day it would crash down and disappear from the city's skyline completely — in fact, the city had believed so almost since its foundation.

However, an artist named Nebuchadnezzar became fascinated with the majesty of the tower, fascinated to such an extent that he hoped to personally climb to its cloud-wreathed peak. The reason for this stemmed from his childhood.

The young Nebuchadnezzar was a talented artist. In his early years, he once vividly painted, on the very apex of the crowning dome of the city's central shrine, a vision of the gods dancing gracefully amidst moonlit mountains during the dawn of the world. Even those knowledgeable sages from Thran could not help but stop in praise and wonder. Yet this proud young man was left unsatisfied by such trifles. He became obsessed with those magnificent, delightful, mysterious, and dreamlike experiences, and so was eager to create indescribably beautiful pictures as yet unknown to the world.

It was to this purpose that he joined other adventure-seeking youths in their journeys through the gloomy dead woods north of the city and approached the much-avoided tower for a closer look. This was an experience full of gloomy, horrific, and other fantastic sensations, yet at the same time also giving rise to countless other novel inspirations and fancies. When the time came for him to gaze upon those wilted vines entangling the grotesque stone statues lying in the shade of dark trees, Nebuchadnezzar thought of enormous wyrms — never seen before by human eyes — slithering through thick piles of bones down in the Vale of Pnath. And when he looked up at the base of the giant tower underneath the still grey sky, Nebuchadnezzar also envisioned those towering basalt columns that rise up by the great waterfall at the edge of the world. Following this, he brushed the timeworn surface of the tower with his own hand, carefully studying the chiseled markings that had been left upon it. Those markings — which could not possibly have been completed by man's hand alone — had already been left imperfect by the wind's erosion, leaving only shallow traces of what had once been. These barely discernible patterns and lines were difficult to explain. It was almost as if they represented an aesthetic concept that was previously unknown to him, but one that filled him with an incomparable curiosity due to their harmony with a certain beautiful essence. During this time, however, Nebuchadnezzar still did not climb the tower, not even daring to linger by the tower for too long. His thrill-seeking expedition neither revealed any further secrets nor forged deeper memories within him. The only subtle traces were the occasional flashes of inspiration that revealed themselves within his paintings.

In his twenty-eighth year, Nebuchadnezzar boarded a sailboat to Hlanith in his pursuit of ever-more fabulous, novel, and pleasing experiences. He bade farewell to the city of his birth and took the first step in his glorious quest to seek out miracles. He once stood on the side of a sailboat, gazing across the sea at a forest of black towers protruding from the ominous fog of Dylath-Leen. He once strolled languidly beside the twin headlands of crystal that guard the port of Sona-Nyl. He even once climbed up cliffs made of glass toward the quaint little town of Ilek-Vad, whence he was able to look in bewilderment at the glimmering sea below. In addition to these, he also visited many people, hearing many an incredible story and anecdote from them. The sages who lived in the white city of Thran told him about the secrets of the gods. The drunks gathered in the taverns of Hlanith babbled stories of the mirages seen by sailors whilst at sea. Even when he boarded a ship to Serannian — that city of legend which floats beyond the boundaries of sea and sky within the ethereal coast — to meet with the great king who had created Ooth-Nargai, the legendary monarch also spoke of the outermost void where no dreams reach.

The young artist greedily drew inspiration and sustenance from these incredible views and rumors, and utilized his exceptional talent to create beautiful paintings of increasing sophistication. Gradually, he earned himself the highest of reputations. Poets struggled to describe in verse the glorious scenery that flowed from his brush; followers traversed the seas in succession in order to gather by the artist's side so that they could hear the tales of his travels and see his entrancing works. Even those wise sages — learned and proficient in the ancient books — were willing to descend from their high towers to share with him hidden secrets unknown to the common man.

Yet as time went by, other things began to take root and subconsciously entangle his mind. Imperceptibly, the mellow wines could remind him only of the intoxicating fragrance of his native land, the exquisite gardens of the royal palaces paled in comparison to the green grass that he had played in as a child, and those magnificent cities replete with exotic sights were now checkered with the shadows of his hometown's alleyways. The feeling of homesickness pawed at his heartstrings like a gentle animal, softly but stubbornly.

During this time, he had a dream.

Nebuchadnezzar would forever remember that carnival night he spent in the City of Art. Wild fun with his followers amidst the bright sounds of the lute; filling a wine cup carved from alabaster from the wine vat and drinking it whole; throwing large chunks of peyote wood into the bonfire, then laughing uncontrollably amid the psychedelic gases emitted by the burning of the wood. In the end, they stretched themselves out beneath a marble colonnade of purest white, gazing up into the deep dark night sky and slowly drifting off into sleep.

At first he did not know where he was, only that he felt boundless and unlimited space all around him. Above his head was a deep blue sky absent the slightest imperfection, pure as the most perfect crystal. Beneath him rolled a magnificent vista of unbroken cloud, piled in great mountain ranges. Although he was not standing on the summit of these cloud mountains, the loftiest peaks made of thin clouds were still far, far below. Nebuchadnezzar could not feel his own body and thought he had become like one of the spirits of myth and legend. He walked, floated, or flew in the transparent space of the empty air in a manner that was incomprehensible even to himself. Not the slightest sound could be heard — the world seemed to be immobile — and he wandered aimlessly within this realm.

Before long he felt the wind, or at least saw the blowing of the wind. Those majestic mountains of cloud began to revolve and change into weird and wonderful shapes. Slowly they spread out, like a vast and endless stage being revealed as the curtain slowly opened, revealing a hidden beauty of a kind he had never seen before. At first it was an expanse of beautiful soft green, a vast plain and an elegant valley with dark green forests and dotted with blue-grey cliffs. Next he saw a shining ribbon, shrinking and tapering its winding way through the middle of the enchanting greenery. He quickly realized that it was a wide river, before it finally joined with a seemingly boundless dark blue water. Then, as the distant clouds calmly dispersed, he saw the boundary between water and sky at the farthest extent of his sight and how the two different shades of blue gradually became brighter, converging together to form a slender cream-colored line. The god of the bright day was driving his blazing chariot out from the middle of this thin line.

As the nearby clouds began to fade to the sides and revealed the most essential part of this beautiful picture, the young artist could not help but hold his breath. He saw his own hometown slowly appear beneath his feet. Though there were no specific details that allowed him to recognize his hometown immediately, his every thought cried out to him that this was so. Every little element in the elegant and adorable grey-white city far below him fitted perfectly with the beauty of his memories. The light of dawn bathed the entire city in a bright and poignant glow. He saw the white marble fountain spraying spring water in the smooth-granite square, scattering colorful prismatic light in all directions. Several alabaster bridges stretched across the calm waters, shyly reaching out from the green shade of the riverbank. Graceful trees, colorful flowerbeds, and bright white statues were neatly arranged on both sides of the city's ancient streets and alleyways like cobwebs. The dome of the temple sparkled softly in the fresh morning light. It was heaven on earth: a heavenly reflection used by the gods to transcend any of the crafts of mortal man.

When he awoke again, Nebuchadnezzar felt at a loss. Everything seemed to have lost its color. His mind ached with an intense, incessant, maddening desire at the loss of such dazzling things. The artist picked up his brush and tried his utmost to depict this incomparably mesmerizing dream, but to no avail. He could still remember the scenery, the composition, the amazing depth and color — everything seemed to have been burned into his mind. Yet he could not depict them with his actual brush. It was as if the ability needed for this type of painting transcended human skill and entered into divine territory. Nebuchadnezzar painted seven scrolls in succession; each piece alone would have been enough to excite the most discerning of connoisseurs and fill them with words of praise, but all he could feel was utter inadequacy. Compared to that refined and vivid dreamworld these paintings appeared both depressing and dull, like a pathetic imitation created by an infant trying to copy the works of a great master. By the time he lifted his brush to begin work on his eighth painting, the artist already felt only despair, a sense of empty exhaustion. He sadly recalled the ancient legends — those legends which claimed that mankind could sometimes cast off their mortal earthly shells during sleep and even explore the realm of the gods.

The desperate artist began to constantly repeat the actions of that night, again and again drinking in the psychedelic gases to fall into a stupor, hoping by this way to re-enter that unearthly, wonderful world. He gained nothing, except for a hangover. Therefore, the helpless Nebuchadnezzar turned his hopes toward the gods themselves. He spent copious amounts of time offering up pious prayers and supplications to all the gods he knew; but the gods were hidden and silent, unwilling to show the slightest pity or compassion. Finally, the despondent artist had no choice but to give up the eighth picture, and to bury that beautiful dream deep within his heart. The goddess of inspiration, however, had changed into a most formidable temptress. The impression left by that enchanting dream occupied his mind and refused to leave. No matter how hard he tried to paint other things, his efforts all unknowingly became failed attempts to outline that world. By the time this had left him completely drained and exhausted, the artist remembered the black tower that lay to the north of his hometown.

He boarded a large merchant ship that had sailed from Hlanith and was able to procure a brass pocket telescope with the ship's first mate in exchange for a sketch of a beautiful girl. With this telescope, Nebuchadnezzar was able to carefully examine the tower in the north for the first time. Happily, he discovered that the degree of wind erosion to the body of the great stone tower was far less severe than he had imagined, as if some kind of magic had protected it. Time itself had lost its destructive ability. The surface of its thick stone walls contained not a single window, nor the trace of any blocked window. The entire tower seemed to be like a giant stone column planted between heaven and earth. Yet Nebuchadnezzar never saw the top of the tower. Even on the clearest afternoon, the telescope elucidated only the length of the vaulting tower, which rose until it shrank to an inscrutable point at the limit of his vision. Regardless, the artist still firmly believed the roof of the tower held some kind of window from which to look down. Perhaps the builders had left behind a small door when building the canopy, or maybe the wind had caused the roof to collapse and had left behind a hole exposed to the sky.

So, one afternoon in early summer, Nebuchadnezzar once again set foot on the land of his hometown. He returned to those quaint and elegant streets, strolled once more along the white river embankment that lay beneath the lovely shade, and lingered in the granite square as charming fragrances wafted through the air. Both these familiar and unfamiliar sights soothed his yearning and tormented heart like a fine mellow wine. Yet these intimate close-ups of such wondrous things could not compare to the soul-wrenching shock, nor the serenity and grandeur, of the harmonious beauty he had overlooked from his distant vantage point in the dreamworld. Nevertheless, Nebuchadnezzar was not disappointed. From the moment he caught sight of that nameless tower looming in the blue northern sky, the artist believed with even greater certainty that he would gaze upon that indescribable scene once more — as long as he could reach that unseen peak.

On a cool morning, Nebuchadnezzar shouldered his baggage and set forth upon his dream path. He brought with him a lantern, spare kerosene, flint, an ample supply of dry food, and — since he had still not given up on his plan to depict that astonishing scene — an easel and a full set of painting tools. He even brought with him a set of rudimentary rock-climbing equipment, as used by quarry miners, just in case. When walking upstream along the meandering and flat green embankments of the Aran River, he encountered, by the front of the shoal, several shepherds hurrying their flock forward in the direction of the rich pastures on the opposite riverbank. They exchanged a few simple greetings, but the artist made no mention of his journey. After bidding farewell to the shepherds, he left the cool riverbank and headed toward that grey and withered forest. Once more he saw those strange and grotesque statues, still lying quietly in the forest as before. Yet he no longer feared these things as he had done when young. Compared to some of the dangers he had since encountered, he reckoned these twisted statues as far less terrible, even ridiculous. Before long he had traversed the grey forest and climbed the small gravel hills beyond which not a blade of grass grew. As the risen sun crested the low mountains, he arrived at the foot of the soaring tower.

The magnificent creation, built from huge monolithic stone pieces, was just as spectacular and awe-inspiring as he remembered. In comparison, he felt like a mere ant crouching at the foot of a giant, helpless to attempt anything but a fearful glance upward at the peak which lay beyond his field of vision. The entrance to the giant tower was an open hole: there was no gate ahead to open or close, nor was there any evidence that such a facility had ever existed. Though the square entrance was over ten feet high, it appeared laughably small compared to the height of the giant tower as a whole. This mood of unease did nothing to deter Nebuchadnezzar's footsteps. The artist used a flint to light his lantern, and then walked resolvedly into the building that likely no man had set foot in for hundreds of thousands of years.

A thick layer of dust covered the ground at the base of the tower, and even the air itself seemed to become heavy and suffocating. However, Nebuchadnezzar could not smell the decaying odor that normally accompanied old buildings. He realized that the giant tower might not have used any wooden materials during its construction; or that perhaps any wooden structure had already long ago rotted completely and dissolved into dust. After the artist had looked all around, he found a route leading upward. It was an enormous sturdy staircase that spiraled upward like a long snake crawling along the inner edge of the tower. Each step of the staircase was immensely wide; slightly higher than those of a normal staircase but not particularly steep. Slender and delicate handrails appeared to have been installed where the staircase met with the inner wall of the tower, but these had not stood the test of time. Only a few obscure pedestals remained to suggest any trace of their past existence.

Nebuchadnezzar thus raised his lantern, and step by

step climbed the stone staircase. A magnificently deco-rated mural that had long been obscured by the winds of time followed his footsteps as he climbed up against the inner wall of the tower. It was a series of abstract decorations consisting of lines and dots. It seemed simple on the surface, but it continued to extend repeatedly upward in accordance with some elusive and fantastical law. Every forty-second step he would find a flat stone platform — seemingly some type of resting place — and the walls of these platforms were engraved with huge murals equal to his own height. Yet the artist had no way to understand the hidden meaning they sought to reveal to him. The murals were mostly engraved with rows of bizarre symbols and basic geometric patterns and curves. Nebuchadnezzar thought that the symbols might be a form of language — perhaps acting as an explanation or title to the murals — but these symbols often occupied a large part of the mural space. Though the geometric patterns were very plain and regular, there was absolutely no way to speculate on their meaning. And yet, thought the artist, the cone must have held an extraordinary meaning for the creator of the giant tower. Out of all the geometric patterns that were depicted in the murals, cones — especially flared cones — accounted for the vast majority. During his ascent he also passed several sections of an onyx handrail that had not yet been completely destroyed; he even stopped deliberately to study closely the fine patterns carved upon them.

It was a hard but enjoyable journey. The hope of seeing once more the beauty of the glorious scenery witnessed in his dream drove him to climb upward as if unaware of his tiredness. When he did finally collapse in exhaustion on the surface of one of the platforms, the light from the entrance below had entirely disappeared. The artist did not know if this was because it was already dark outside, or if it was because he had climbed too great a height. Whatever the explanation, he did not possess the energy to further ponder this question. After eating a few things, Nebuchadnezzar curled up in fatigue against the wall and sensed himself falling into the dreamlands. That fervent desire which had spurred him in his climb upward now also began to quietly seep into his dreams, revealing itself to him in concrete imagery. He dreamt of floating freely in the sky; gracefully flying over vast plains, beautiful river valleys, soaring mountains, and tempting forests. Though these visions were clearly born from his usual imagination and far less detached than what he had seen in that singular dream, they still gave him a feeling of immense satisfaction.

When Nebuchadnezzar awoke again, he ate some more and then continued to climb the spiral staircase. He would, from time to time, move his head to look up or down the shaft in the middle of the staircase, yet no matter which direction he looked there was only an endless darkness, as though staring into two deep bottomless wells arrayed in opposition. Later, he realized that the steps accompanied by handrails were gradually increasing until they steadily became continuous. The gaps left behind by destruction were becoming rarer; as if time itself had begun to lose its power toward the top of this endless staircase. In this manner he continued his ascent until he collapsed from exhaustion a second time. Even so, his surroundings betrayed no change: he had not passed any windows or holes that opened to the outside, nor were there any signs of the peak.

This discouraged the artist, but he faced a much more serious problem than he had anticipated: because the incredible length of the staircase far exceeded his expectations, Nebuchadnezzar quickly realized that he did not possess enough kerosene. If he were to use up his final drop of oil during his ascent, then he would be scrabbling in the dark for sure when the time came for him to return to the ground. This would be a very arduous task, but what really terrified the artist was that even if he burnt his last drop of oil climbing this strange tower he still might not necessarily have arrived at the top. He thought that since his reserves of dry food far exceeded those of his kerosene, he could most probably continue to climb upward in the dark. Or he could give up on his plans to ascend the tower, and go back to plan again. While considering these two conflicting thoughts, the artist extinguished his lantern, and within the deep darkness drifted off into his second slumber.

When he awoke for the second time, Nebuchadnezzar mechanically lit his lantern and began his climb once more, deliberating not one moment further upon the serious problem that he had pondered before his sleep. His crazed and stubborn desire to return to that world of supreme beauty pushed him ceaselessly in his ascent, overcoming even his own ability to think. And so, he continued upward for around half a day until finally he reached the moment his oil ran out. The last ray of light in the lantern seemed to be smothered by the darkness, and after swaying for a while it disappeared completely. His surroundings were plunged into an unbearable darkness and silence. His spirit appeared to have detached itself from all of the senses he depended on, and he had been submerged into a vat of sticky tar. Nebuchadnezzar's sense of time began to blur, and he felt like he had stood in the same place for both an infinite period of time ... and the blink of an eye. When the artist came to his senses he groped and clambered to the edge of the steps, tossing the now-useless lantern down the shaft that ran down the middle of the spiral staircase, before sitting numbly on the stairs.

He waited for a long time. Though his concept of time had shattered and stretched indefinitely within the absolute darkness — he still thought it was an infinitely long time: long enough for a gentle breeze to grind the legendary Diamond Mountain that stands in the icy wastelands into fine powder, or for an eternal flame to burn dry all the water in all the oceans of the world drop by drop — he never heard the sound of the lantern hitting the ground. Thus, he rose, and filled with an inexplicable fear he carried on groping his way onward.

He stumbled up in this way for two more days — if the cycle of tiredness, sleep, then waking up to continue climbing till exhaustion returned could be called a day. For the majority of the time Nebuchadnezzar felt manipulated like a marionette, with no feeling, no plan, no thought and no soul. Sometimes, weird and grotesque thoughts would erupt spontaneously in his mind, like anomalous waves from a pool of stagnant water. Sometimes, he faintly imagined he had been climbing the tower for his entire life. The mountains, rivers, plains, oceans, skies, and beautiful dreamscapes outside the tower all seemed impossibly distant and vague — nothing more than an illusory fantasy. Sometimes, he wondered in confusion whether or not he was already blind, or if there was no light in the world at all. Sometimes he would timidly conclude that gloomy and mischievous gods hid in the unseen darkness, pointing at him and snickering soundlessly. The only thing he knew for sure was that the carvings, handrails and steps around him seemed to grow newer and fresher as he ascended; gradually losing the round smoothness that years of abrasion ought to have brought about, instead becoming straight and hard.

When he awoke in the tower for the fifth time, the world seemed to have undergone some miraculous transformation. When Nebuchadnezzar looked up unwittingly, he felt that there was almost a faint hint of light illuminating the very edge of his sight. At first he thought it must have been an illusion — he had experienced countless instances already. Yet when he made his way up through several circuits of the spiral, the tiny speck of light so infinitely far above began to become clearly visible. There was no further doubt: he had indeed seen some kind of exit. He suddenly experienced a great hope and strength. Under the encouragement of this small ray of light he accelerated his climb. Then, after climbing innumerable steps, the artist finally saw the source of the light in all truth and reality. It was an immensely large exit similar in his memory to the entrance below, and like that entrance was devoid of any gate to open or close. The glow of twilight penetrated through the open portal and illuminated by the exit a spacious platform with carved railings that was connected to the end of this long spiral staircase.

Nebuchadnezzar rested on the stairs for a while, and then with difficulty ascended to the platform beyond the exit he had dreamt of finding. Confusion, surprise, astonishment, terror, and all of his other entangled emotions swirled and rushed together within Nebuchadnezzar's head, until the essence of fear of the vastness before him overwhelmed all other feelings and pinned him firmly to the ground.

It was not the blue skies of his dream that appeared on the other side of the portal, but a frightening expanse of bright stars. Yet this was not a singular galaxy adorned with star clusters, but in fact a vast sea of light formed from countless galaxies merging with one another. Amidst the bright starlight even the darkness had lost its place. It had been severed, removed and scattered in all directions till it became just a faint spot on the cold light canopy of the sky. Neither Nebuchadnezzar nor anyone he knew had ever seen so many stars, so the scene he beheld gave him the illusion of transcending this vulgar world. Their number would dwarf the total of all the water droplets within the three oceans, and would leave aghast those philosophers in their masoned cities who had become complacent over their mastery of infinite numbers. The sages of the city of Ptolemy who had devoted their lives to studying the mysteries of the stars had told him that every star in the night sky meant a whole new world. Nebuchadnezzar felt totally stunned and helpless when he tried to connect this secret with the sight that engulfed him.

He stood there dazed for some time, till slowly he began to notice his surroundings: he was standing on a classical terrace ten square feet in size, with the bizarre spire of the tower towering behind him like a fine needle. The surface of the terrace was laid out in perfectly flat granite slabs that gave no appearance as to having experienced any erosion from the passage of time. Skirting around the edge of the terrace, the delicate guardrail carved from onyx was also clear, elegant and spotless. These familiar things reminded Nebuchadnezzar of his purpose in climbing the tower, so he dragged his feet forward to the edge of the terrace and looked down from the waist-high guardrail, hoping that the familiar and wonderful land below would display its touching beauty beneath the brilliance of the stars.

However, what he saw below the handrail caused him to lose his senses, leaving him faint.

There were no sweeping plains below, no beautiful river valleys, no billowing mountains of cloud. Beneath the handrail was only another expanse of starry sky — as sidereal and as vast as the sky above his head. He saw the huge tower stretching downward; shrinking and tapering from a stone pillar, to a long rope, and finally to a sharp needle, lost amidst a bewildering, bottomless, star-filled abyss.

This confusing scene caused Nebuchadnezzar much unease. He paced back a few steps then sat down on the icy granite terrace, looking up hollowly at the bright stars with no idea at all. Then something else caught his attention. He saw, in the zenith of the heavens, that where the tower's spire pointed to was a circular patch of blackness. It was about the same size as the full moon when seen from the ground, but Nebuchadnezzar didn't know what it was, nor could he even find the words to describe it. However, the artist's keen sense of discernment told him that it was not the color of the night sky as usually seen from the ground. It was more like a hole or a vortex wrought into the fabric of the sky. Anything close to it became distorted; even the stars were torn into a mottled strip of light that surrounded the menacing silhouette. What it showed was nothingness: the color behind the sky. That place was more horrifying than the darkness of the common world; it seemed that even light could not escape it.

Then, as he focused further on the stars above his head, the artist beheld an even more fearful sight — he saw the movement of the stars. The astrologers of the city of Ptolemy had once mentioned the movements and changes of the stars among their whispers, but those changes were as slow as those of the oceans drying into mulberry fields. At first, he felt that all the stars were gathering together in that patch of blackness in the zenith above. However, he was then aware that these stars were not actually moving in the same direction — but converging in on each other, as if the entire celestial sphere was gradually deflating and causing the stars upon it to become closer and closer. This incredible transformation was accelerating at a rate visible to the naked eye. Nebuchadnezzar saw that the small specks of dark space were progressively disappearing as the nebulas and the Milky Way merged. The whole sky became brighter and brighter, until the entire canopy of the starry heavens became one glorious sea of light. Though he was infinitely far away, Nebuchadnezzar felt that the whole world was about to unavoidably collapse upon him with increasing speed. Only the strange circle in the sky's zenith was left dark and without light. The all-encompassing light intensified, finally converging into a single piercing screen of white light, burning and roasting so that Nebuchadnezzar had no choice but to cover his eyes from the hundreds of billions of stars that seemed to flare around him.

Then, in one particular instant, the countless stars and worlds crushed together seemed to have arrived at a certain threshold. A strong beam of light swept across the entire universe. Even when the artist used both of his hands to cover his eyes, a stream of glaring whiteness scorched his tightly closed eyes. The world began to fall apart in an explosion that almost drove him out of the tower. His surroundings dimmed, though the light was still dazzling. Once accustomed to the light, the artist opened his eyes once again to check if he was really alive after experiencing such terrible destruction — but the fate of being cursed by eternity had cast him into a nightmare.

These scenes had destroyed everything he understood about space, so he did not know if he had really witnessed these things, or even how he had seen them. He saw countless universes, like fruits bearing branches, hanging in the formless void. He also saw all the sights in all the universes; their expansion and contraction, their explosion and annihilation. Yet most horrifying was not the vast emptiness that broke the minds of men. He looked up to see that far, far beyond the orderly universe, beyond even time itself, lay an even more frenzied chaos. The furious and ever-changing destructive powers writhed and remained within the infinite madness at the center. This last scene was the final straw that caused Nebuchadnezzar to snap. He ran behind and escaped it all, fleeing back to the familiar darkness of the tower's interior. Behind him the stars of the sky were gradually forming and spreading out. Matter and light were reborn into what the universe had once been in the past: endless stars, endless suns, endless worlds crawling with life....

He knew not how long he had run, nor how far he had traveled. By the time his senses recovered, instinct had already spurred him far down the dark path. Once more he was plunged all alone into the thick, suffocating darkness, though this time when running the bruises and wounds incurred from tumbling from a great height made everything worse. But even so, Nebuchadnezzar still felt that all this was much more comforting than the scene above. Finally, he collapsed in exhaustion upon one of the platforms, the light from the tower's peak having already disappeared. He stayed in the bosom of the total darkness trying to comfort himself with memories of that sweet dreamland, but the only things that came to his mind were the stars of the sky, the darkness of nihility, the universe full of branches, and the furious flailing of terminal chaos.

He curled up in a ball, buried his face in his palms, and cried silently.

It took the artist five more days to emerge gropingly from the tower. The wounds on his body had left him powerless and tired, and the dreadful sights embedded in his mind caused him to tremble uncontrollably. He struggled his way through the grey withered forest in his attempt to return to the warm city where he had been born and raised, seeking the last consolation available in this vast universe. Yet when he crossed out of the valley from the meandering Aran River, he stopped in his tracks. He saw a vast rolling plain and tumbling hills, the Aran River flowing through the green meadows, several herdsmen leading their flocks across the shallow riverbanks nearby ... but the beloved and familiar city — his home — had disappeared. There were no quaint streets, no elaborate buildings, no crowds of people coming and going. The whole city seemed to have been erased from this vast canvas by a giant hand — wiped clean completely without a wreck, ruin, or even a single brick remaining. The artist had lost his last hope and finally fainted in abject despair.

Some of the herdsmen came over to help the stranger who had suddenly appeared. They had never heard of the city uttered by the stranger when they asked where he had come from. The man told them of his experiences; he described the route he had taken from his hometown to climb the tower, the scenes he had witnessed on its peak, and the preposterous situation he had been plunged into after escaping it. Yet to the herdsmen these crazy stories sounded like the ravings of a frightened madman. Not long after, a peculiar story began to spread in the neighboring region. It spoke of a reckless and crazed fool who attempted to climb the peak of the tower and enter the realm of the gods. Yet nobody knew what he had seen, as when the fool came down, nobody could understand the absurdities he described.

After many years had passed, brave explorers excavated precious ore along the banks of the Aran River, followed by others who flocked there to lay the foundations of a beautiful and beloved city.

North of the city there lay a black tower.

*The End*

As incredible and fantastic his story was, I had no reason to believe that there was any untruth to what the Dreamer was telling me. It is true that there are Dreamlands on the opposite side of the veil called reality; at times these lands even leak and merge with lands from our own waking existence. I have heard it said that the Plateau of Leng, which exists in our world as a cold and inaccessible desert plateau, exists simultaneously in the Dreamlands as an unreachable land full of horrible stone villages, which no healthy folk visit and whose evil fires are seen at night from afar.

"I have had other dreams," continued the Dreamer, "Dreams of strange high houses in the mist, other gods, and the doom that came to Sarnath. I have seen...."

At any other time I may have been inclined to hear more of the Dreamer's tales, but at that moment I happened to glimpse a small movement from within the wooden box and I motioned the Dreamer to be quiet. Of all the objects in the ancient box, this one was probably the most curious — and certainly the most alarming — for I knew what it was. My obvious distaste for the object in the box must have been apparent, for one of my guests offered up his voice.

*"It is still moving?" asked the Historian, for it was he who spoke.*

*"Yes," I said. "It moves."*

*"Does it grow?"*

*"It is safe for now. It cannot leave its container."*

*I did not raise this particular object from the box, for unlike the scroll and the painting, this vile, unnatural creation filled me with loathing and I felt more than an inkling of fear intermingled with my abhorrence. It continued to wriggle and squirm in its container in defiance of me, so I closed the box and decided to leave the room, heading into the cool night air to recollect my senses.*

*Stepping out of the farmhouse, I was relieved to feel the cold surround my body, washing away the stuffiness and heat of the room. Above me lay the infinite gulf of space, comforting in its boundlessness and icy nihility, the memory of Nebuchadnezzar and the starry abyss he encountered fresh in my mind. Instinctively I scanned the heavens, seeking amid the pinpricks of twinkling cosmic light the constellation of Ursa Major. The winter wind gnawed at my body as I thought of strange dark orbs at the very rim of our solar system, and what lay even farther beyond, out in the voids past the universe, where chaos roils and churns upon itself.*

> *I have seen the dark universe yawning,*
> *Where the black planets roll without aim;*
> *Where they roll in their horror unheeded,*
> *without knowledge or luster or name.*

*Someone told me these words long ago, another of my*

*many guests, though I remembered little about him except that he had been a writer bestowed with considerable love for his craft. Refreshed by the night air, I returned once more inside.*

*I did not reopen the box for now, but instead turned to the Historian, who harbored just as much fear toward the grotesque black object that had found its way into his possession as I did. He had been relieved to relinquish ownership of the monstrosity when I had first made my presence known to him; and like my other guests, he had damaged his sanity by witnessing strange things that no mortal man should ever see. Though I knew infinitely more as to the true nature of the dark wiggling thing trapped within the box than he did, it was most important that I learn more about how he had first encountered it and what he knew of its history.*

*"Tell me how you found this … thing," I commanded, but the Historian remained silent. Not totally insensitive to his fear of the ghastly black object, I decided to adopt a different approach, one that would appeal to his historian's innate sense of curiosity.*

*"Do not be afraid. Let us use this opportunity to learn from one another during the time that has been granted us. To us, as to only a few men on this earth, there will be opened up gulfs of time and space and knowledge far beyond anything within the conception of human science and philosophy. Does that offer you no comfort?"*

*My cajoling achieved its desired effect, for after a few moments of silence the Historian spoke quietly.*

*"It found its way to me when I was investigating the history of a strange incident that occurred in Qingdao.*

I'm a local historian of the city; when I first heard of this incident, I started to carry out my own investigations."

"Carry on," I said as I sat back and listened to the soft voice of the Historian, his words intertwined with the hideous hints of vibration that permeated this darkened room.

# Black Taisui

RESIDENTS of Qingdao or attentive followers of local news may have heard of the affair I wish to discuss. On the 14th of August 2013, during a routine fire-safety inspection, a worker from the residential committee of Shinan District's University Road discovered a heavily decomposed corpse by a small building inside the courtyard of Number 5 Longkou Road. After receiving the report, the Jiangsu Road Police Station immediately dispatched a team to cordon off the area and launch a detailed investigation to gather evidence. The preliminary findings of the case were published in the local papers, which are not difficult to find. In sum, the deceased was Lao Mingchang, a sixty-nine-year-old resident of the house. The police found no traces of any break-in during their on-site inspection, nor was there evidence of stolen property, so the cause of death was initially determined to be natural. Yet those who have had the opportunity to read the investigation file in detail, or to visit Longkou Road and hear the local gossip, may uncover a few curious inconsistencies.

According to the investigation records, officers found the deceased in the living room on the ground floor, but the foul stench was strong enough to fill the entire building. The circumstances of the scene were perturbing; the corpse had almost completely decayed into a pool of dark mucus. Only by examining the bones could one discern a human figure. Common sense would dictate that such a level of decay could be possible only after several weeks or months, but when interviewed by the police, neighboring residents claimed they had spoken with Lao only a few days prior to the body's discovery. An autopsy corroborated their testimony: there were no signs of larvae breeding within the corpse, indicating that the deceased's actual time of death was much shorter than it appeared. The appraisal report emphasized that the atrocious condition of the body made inference of the exact cause of death impossible, and yet bones collected on-site exhibited no signs of external trauma, somewhat eliminating the possibility of violent death.

The forensics doctor also analyzed the mucus collected from the body and determined it to be a mixture of bodily fluids and putrefied organs. This was — unlike the soft dissolving of tissue commonly caused by bacteria — more akin to the result of some rapid chemical or biological process. The conclusions gave the authorities reason to suspect that the results may have been the symptoms of certain malignant diseases. A low-profile investigation of infectious diseases was conducted in the surrounding area, though a rigorous pathological examination determined that the phenomenon had not occurred as a result of any known pathogens — and the neighbors elucidated stranger phenomena than just the body. A mere two nights before the body was discovered, several residents reported hearing a shrill, oddly rhythmic whistle emanating from the building where Lao lived. Others spoke of an unsettling young man who Lao had developed a close relationship with several months previously, yet police were unable to find any footage of suspicious people moving around the compound on surveillance footage from the days preceding the event. Due to the lack of substantive clues or evidence, the police eventually tabled the evidence and sealed the file with a verdict of non-violent death.

Speaking frankly, the deceased was no more than a childless old eccentric who rarely spoke to his neighbors (most of whom dismissed the case as an unfortunate tragedy). According to the will found in the room, Lao's collection of books, notes, and assorted documents were to be donated to his former work unit, the Shandong Provincial Cultural Relics and Archaeology Institute. Any proceeds from sale of the remaining property were to be donated to various heritage conservation foundations. Since no legal heirs were forthcoming, the estate sale went relatively smoothly, and things ought to have ended there.

However, it arose that this case indirectly resulted in a series of second-order consequences. Lao Mingchang's diaries and documents, for example, sparked considerable heated argument upon their arrival at the Shandong Provincial Cultural Relics and Archaeology Institute, although the pointless disputes never made it beyond a small circle of staff. In February

2014 — four months after the bequeathed items had been transferred to the archaeological institute — a number of researchers from the institute returned to the former residence of the late Lao Mingchang, carefully inspected the entire house, and then removed several crates of documents. One month later, the Qingdao Municipal Public Security Bureau mobilized a police squad in a sudden raid on the area — mainly in the neighborhood of Signal Hill Park — but did not comment on the reasons or results of the exercise. At the beginning of April, the Housing and Construction Bureau of Shinan District conducted a comprehensive inspection of Lao's former home and declared it a hazardous edifice, which revoked the transaction permit for the house, meaning it was no longer available for residence until proper repairs were undertaken.

The reader must make up his own mind as to the reality behind this sequence of events. As a participant who has cross-checked all available evidence and thoroughly analyzed the contents of the surviving documents, I will attempt to give a somewhat complete narrative of the whole affair, based on the protagonist's first-hand diaries and documents, combined with my own circumstances and speculation.

## 2.

Although Lao lived in Qingdao, he was born in Chongqing on September 20, 1942, an only child. His father, Lao Chuanlin, had once worked as an aide-de-camp for General Tang Junyao.[1] Nothing is known about his mother, Chen Yu, other than that she was from Fengtian.[2] In October 1942, when Lao Mingchang was three years old, his father followed General Tang to Qingdao to begin forcing the Japanese army's surrender. In February 1946, after the Qingdao Office of the Deputy-Command of the Eleventh Military Region was abolished, Lao Chuanlin tried to find an opportunity to transfer under the leadership of Li Xianliang[3] and bring his wife and son to Qingdao. In January 1949, Chen Yu died in an accident. After the end of the Jinan campaign in April, Lao Chuanlin brought his six-year-old son and surrendered to the People's Liberation Army before settling down in Jinan. Lao Chuanlin passed away from an illness in 1963. During the Cultural Revolution, Lao Mingchang was sent down to the countryside in 1966 to work as a farmer in Licheng and suffered immensely due to his family background. He retook the college entrance examination in 1977 and was admitted to the history department of Shandong University, then joined the Shandong Provincial Cultural Relics and Archaeology

1    Tang Junyao (1899–1967) was a Republican general born in Liaoning Province. He oversaw the Qingdao area after the war against the Japanese. He moved to Hong Kong in 1948 after Communist advances in the Civil War.

2    Fengtian is now known as Shenyang — the capital of Liaoning Province. It is also known by its Manchu name of Mukden.

3    Li Xianliang (1904–?) was the Republican mayor of Qingdao from 1945 till he fled to Taiwan in 1949.

Institute in 1984 after completing his master's degree, working there until his retirement in 2007.

For health reasons, Lao moved to Qingdao in the spring of 2008 and rented a room in a five-story building on Yushan Road. The small building was tucked away on a hillside situated in the northwest of Xiao Yushan,[4] next door to Qingdao Ocean University. I have walked there many times; it is a charming place to live. The surroundings are quiet and peaceful, and few vehicles pass through. The entrance of the building leads onto Yushan Road as it winds down from the top of Xiao Yushan. The cream-colored fence of the university campus, perpetually smothered with creeping ivy, lines the opposite side of the street. Quaint and elegant brick-red campus rooftops in the European style loom over the lush walls, creating an adorable little corner that invites one to explore deeper. Downhill from the narrow Yushan Road, a small bend leads to the main entrance of Qingdao Ocean University. Through the main entrance is a stretch of verdant pine trees and bushes, and once past the bushes there stands a European-style building that was constructed during the Japanese occupation. It has granite walls with a beige-colored façade, a typical European tiled roof in orange and red, chic curved ornamentation, and a flat-topped tower of mixed Eastern and Western architectural style that stands in the middle. After passing through the university gate and continuing along the outer wall, you will arrive at a

4    Xiao Yushan literally means "Little Fish Hill." It is a pleasant park in the center of Qingdao overlooking the sea.

crossroads. South from the crossroads — past several more modern-style buildings — there is a lively and popular beach; to the east you may follow the quiet alleyways and the sycamore trees, eventually entering an old world filled with tiled roofs, elegant stone arches, rough granite façades, and cobbled streets. It's a place where time seems to have stood still.

This type of scene, almost unchanged since the early years of the last century, held an even greater meaning for Lao Mingchang. He remembered his father once saying that he and his grandfather Lao Siwei had been born in Qingdao back when the city was still a German concession. Thus, the ancient edifices that had witnessed his ancestors a hundred years previously set his imagination alight. Since he had never married or borne children, a lineage rooted in the hearts of all Chinese people gradually manifested in another manner: he began to become deeply fascinated in his own family history, and increasingly desired to learn more about his ancestors … though this proved a less than easy task. Although his grandfather had been born in Qingdao, when he was five or six years old his great-grandfather had taken him to the northeast, where he had been entrusted to some business acquaintances. Due to the turbulence of those times his grandfather's relationship with his family was swiftly disconnected, leaving his grandfather without any knowledge of his family's earlier generations. In addition, his grandfather passed away at a very early age, meaning that Lao Mingchang received even fewer memories than usual from his ancestors. To this end, he dedicated his time to excavating information concerning his family from the Qingdao Municipal

Archives and the Qingdao Institute of Cultural Relics and Archaeology. In September 2008 he used his work experience at the Shandong Archaeological Institute to land himself a part-time job repairing documents within the municipal archives so that he could access those classified historical documents that had not yet been released for public consumption.

His efforts were not in vain. Lao carefully transcribed all the information he found during this period and compiled it in his own notes: these were the notes that were sent to the Shandong Provincial Cultural Relics and Archaeology Institute after his death to be sorted out by the relevant staff. Though the majority of these notes are overly detailed or trivial, I still believe them essential to compiling a holistic narrative of the events that unfolded, due to the close connection they have with what happened to Lao.

According to the records quoted therein, the Lao family had settled in the town of Yanguan, Zhejiang Province, as early as the mid-Qing dynasty, at which time they were already respected as a local commercial family. During the early years of the reign of the Emperor Xian-feng,[5] one of the family members — the direct ancestor of Lao Mingchang — moved the family to Jimo County within the district of Laizhou,[6] Shandong Province. No reliable records exist as to why the family moved, but looking at the accounts of the Lao family themselves it seemed that the family had accumulated too many enemies in both Zhejiang and Jiangsu provinces and

5    1831–1861.

6    Both Jimo and Laizhou are now part of Qingdao city itself.

so was forced to leave their home. Lao Mingchang's opinion was that this might not have been the exact truth of the matter.

A variety of historical documents mentioned that the family had a very strange habit: certain members of the family would sail out to sea in two or three boats during the evening and not return until days later, in the early hours of the morning. Although they claimed they were only catching fish, they would often return without any fish at all. Given the enormous amount of smuggling that existed around the coastal areas during the mid-to-late Qing dynasty, Lao Mingchang was almost certain his ancestors were involved in this disreputable profession. Perhaps they attracted the attention of the authorities or entered into a feud with rival smugglers — no matter the reason, they had no choice but to leave Zhejiang for Shandong.

Whatever the truth of the matter, the family quickly integrated into the local community. Many historical documents from both Qingdao and Jimo record deeds related to the Lao family, the most impressive of which recount the extraordinary breadth of their knowledge. Documents tell of incidents where members of the Lao family attracted attention by discussing ancient historical affairs or obscure esoteric concerns unbeknown to common folk. Even more extraordinary: not just one or two outstanding members of the family displayed this mastery of arcane wisdom; whether young or old, the whole family could easily discuss historical stories or legends to a level that the average person's comprehension wouldn't even know was true or false. Lao Mingchang had made special note of one extract from

*Assorted Tales from the Pure Heart Studio*, a book that had been left behind by a private tutor named Zhou Yuke. A ten-year-old boy by the name of Lao Hengcai once argued with a storyteller in the street one day over an anecdote about the Ming dynasty general Qi Jiguang. The famous storyteller lost the debate and was left speechless. According to his seniority in the family hierarchy, this Lao Hengcai would have been Lao Mingchang's ancestor to the sixth generation. From literary essays dating from the Emperor Xianfeng's reign, to newspapers following the German occupation of Qingdao, similar stories appear frequently and identically in documents of all ages, varying only in their protagonist. It was as if this profound knowledge was encoded in the Lao family's genes, passed down to each new generation.

Naturally, many people wanted to understand the secret of their erudition, but the reactions of the Lao family were always rather out of the ordinary when faced with such questions. They constantly insisted that there was a way to become immortal in this world, and that they had obtained their knowledge from their immortal ancestors. Although at first people took it for a joke in poor taste, the members of the Lao family all seemed very serious. They would cryptically suggest that not only had the family kept the secret of immortality since antediluvian times, furthermore every family member was an immortal as well ... which was transparently wishful thinking. As a family they were clearly not immortal; they were not even particularly long-lived. So it came that whenever somebody in the family died, spiteful, jealous types never skipped the opportunity to mock them. In order to save face during these situations, the Lao family never held funerals, their coffins buried in secret instead. Nevertheless, some still believed the Lao family's claims — though these people were mostly suspicious and gullible peasants from out of town. They would often gather in the house of the Lao family, assisting them in mysterious rituals or exploring ways to attain immortality. These activities naturally drew considerable criticism, but the unfounded speculations are mostly contradictory.

The Lao family moved from Jimo County to the port of Jiao'ao[7] in early 1898 under a cloud of criticism — though the motivation for the move was mainly business. Germany had occupied Jiao'ao in November 1897. The head of the family at the time — Lao Mingchang's great-grandfather Lao Gelin — established a business as a middleman for foreign traders and became a very well-known translator of German. Lao Gelin had many business partners and an extensive network within Qingdao, meaning that his name had been recorded in various archives. Lao Mingchang developed a much more detailed analysis of his great-grandfather because of this; due also in part to the experiences of this particular ancestor being inextricably linked to what happened to Lao later on. When I checked the documents left behind by Lao, I discovered a black-and-white photograph of Lao Gelin. It was impossible to say how old the photograph was, but Lao Gelin seemed forty to fifty years old. Wearing a light robe and a dark jacket, with a Manchu-style pigtail and skullcap, his face could not

---

7   Sometimes known as Jiaozhou Bay, it is also now a part of Qingdao municipality.

conceal the unease and confusion so often displayed by Chinese of that time when confronted with the camera. The image was quite blurry, due to the age of the photograph; yet the man in that photo gave me an inexplicably uncanny feeling, as though he was someone forgotten long ago, and best left that way.

Lao Gelin purchased a small courtyard during that time beside the Qingdao River, then moved his entire family of more than twenty people — one after the other — to their new home to begin a fresh start. Yet even such a long move could not change the family's old habits. From 1898 to 1905, patrolling German law enforcement would often track down and arrest suspicious persons on the docks at midnight: the archives have more than eight separate records of Lao family members being caught trying to secretly sail their boats out to sea. The Germans also initially suspected that the Lao family was involved in smuggling activities; however, nothing of value was ever found in their boats, nor did the Germans find a secret hiding place of the kind that was often built into smuggling ships. So although German authorities would often detain his family's fishing boats and the people on board, as long as Lao Gelin paid a small fine as guarantee there wasn't too much trouble. In addition, the Lao family also saw a marked increase in the number of people who journeyed to explore the art of immortality, to the extent that they amassed a secret society of considerable size. Sometime around 1903, the group even erected a banner and proclaimed themselves the "School of Longevity," becoming a semi-public sect.

Amidst this series of events, the most interesting one for Lao Mingchang was the attitude of his great-grandfather Lao Gelin. Perhaps in consideration of the feelings of his business partners — especially those devout German Christians — Lao Gelin would always try his best to maintain appropriate boundaries between himself and other members of the family and the School of Longevity. He participated in guilds and commercial associations, donated to charity, and strived to present himself always as an upstanding member of society. In the summer of 1903 he worked with several other businessmen to raise funds for the construction of a stone bridge spanning the Qingdao River that would aid the passage of cargo and dock workers to the port. The bridge was blown up during a battle against the Japanese, but a German journalist photographed a monument inscribed with the names of the bridge's donors, and the name of Lao Gelin can be seen clearly. By 1904 his import-export business occupied a considerable portion of Qingdao Port, and he personally served as director for the Qingdao China Business Bureau. Yet in private Lao Gelin still engaged in occult activities. Surviving letters from that time seem to indicate that Lao Gelin would often ask his business partners to retrieve rare and mysterious books from foreign lands, or assist in the purchase of certain shadowy objects.

Also worth mentioning is something that occurred in 1902. In the autumn of that year, Lao Gelin bought the property surrounding his own small courtyard and hired a group of workers from out of town to expand it. The project lasted nearly three and a half years; and by the spring of 1906 the one-story house had metamorphosed into a high-walled compound. There were a total of three small European-style buildings in the compound, which was laid out in the traditional court-yard style. The entrance led to a spacious courtyard with the main two-story building on the north side and two single-story wings forming a horseshoe. The three buildings were composed of granite from nearby Mount Lao, and rumored to have involved the consultation of a German designer. Many people thought the height of the courtyard walls excessive, hermetically enclosing the entire compound, as if to prevent outsiders from peering in. In addition, a few people familiar with Lao Gelin recounted a very strange phenomenon almost imperceptible to those unacquainted with the family: the earth excavated by Lao Gelin to build his new courtyard seemed far too plentiful. According to their observations, Lao Gelin must have dug an enormous cellar beneath the yard, because the soil transported away by the workers far exceeded that needed for the foundations of the three small buildings. This matter was never settled. First, the walls were too tall to see what transpired within the courtyard during its construction. Second, after the compound was completed, Lao Gelin immediately sent away all of the hired laborers, so there was no way for others to make inquiries of them.

The completion of the new home seemed to mark a new beginning for the Lao family. On the one hand, their surreptitious nocturnal seafaring activities suddenly ceased. Although gossip still persisted about what had taken place in the past, by 1906 the archives of the colonial administration no longer contained any record of the patrol team encountering the Lao family's fishing boats. On the other hand, the School of Longevity expanded vigorously during this period — turning the new family compound into a major hub of activity and attracting many residents of Qingdao to join them. Many neighbors and night watchmen claimed that they saw suspicious people coming in and out of the family compound during the middle of the night, or heard a strange noise emanating from behind those purposefully high walls — like an unintelligible wild cry spouting forth from a crowd, accompanied by a chaotic musical piping and other instruments, ominously evoking the ancient arcane rituals that circulated among secluded coastal villages. Even during the day, passersby often caught wind of a peculiar odor around the Lao family's house, or spied workers carrying sealed boxes into or out of the compound. As for what they contained ... even the workers knew not.

As head of the family, Lao Gelin appeared to have lost the ability to control the situation. A significant number of German businessmen who had contact with him expressed the opinion — publicly and privately — that he should end the disturbing and outlandish activities taking place within his home. Though Lao Gelin replied in agreement to all of their demands, the strange sounds at midnight did not disappear, nor did the number of shady loiterers lingering outside the compound. Later — between the close of 1907 and the beginning of 1909 — the mysterious disappearance of numerous native Qingdao acolytes of the School of Longevity dealt a fatal blow to Lao Gelin's remaining enterprises. Although the German authorities and the police bureau found no clear connection between the disappearances and the Lao family — or the followers of the School of Longevity — many within Qingdao attributed it to them nevertheless, believing it to be part of some enigmatic series of sacrifices. Enlightened individuals dismissed these rumors as mere folktales based on superstition. Then, in 1908, several intellectuals published an article in the opinion column of the *Jiaozhou Daily* accusing Lao Gelin and his associates of "Assembling at night ... dispersing at dawn ... wrongly seeking the secrets of longevity ... luring in the gullible, and murdering them for money."

Under so many burdens, Lao Gelin's businesses collapsed. Most of his friends distanced themselves from him, and those superstitious neighbors viewed the entire Lao family with even greater disdain. His remaining friends, however, noted that the inscrutable businessman seemed no longer to care about public opinion. He became increasingly anxious and fearful but never once mentioned anything untoward about the family or himself. He spent more and more money on apparently meaningless endeavors, such as the collection of old occult books from both nearby and abroad, or meetings with peculiar people. The enterprises that ought to have held his concern all fell to the wayside one by one.

In the early months of 1909, just after the Chinese New Year, Lao Gelin confused everyone by doing another odd thing. He entrusted his most beloved son to the care of a northeastern merchant of medicinal ingredients named Wang Zhicheng, who resided in Fengtian. This child, barely five years of age, was the Lao Siwei who would later become the grandfather of Lao Mingchang. Lao Gelin claimed the reason for the move was to allow Lao Siwei to grow up under the tutelage of Wang Zhicheng and learn the art of the medicine business, but this excuse failed to hold up. The eldest son, Lao Siming — who was already studying the operations of the family businesses — and the sixteen-year-old second son, Lao Side, were both more suitable candidates for the study of medicinal business than a five-year-old child. Idle folk prone to gossip gave their own opinion concerning this irrational arrangement. Most of them thought it was connected to the identity of the boy. Lao Siwei was the son of one of Lao Gelin's concubines who died in childbirth, so his wife had always desired to send him away. Others thought that Lao Gelin was looking for an excuse to get his son out of town to avoid trouble. No one expected that this incident would be the simple prelude to an even bigger transformation.

## 3.

Lao Mingchang did not initially know much about the history of the Lao family after 1909. In all the files collected by the Qingdao Municipal Archives post-1909 there was almost no record at all of Lao Gelin or even the wider family. It was as if the family had abruptly vanished. After further investigation, he managed to find a portentous sentence in a letter written by the medicine merchant Wang Zhicheng — the same Wang Zhicheng who had adopted his grandfather Lao Siwei — to one of his business partners in 1910:

> You will soon hear about what happened to "prosperity." The day "prosperity" entrusted

Siwei to me he already feared a calamity
such as this.

"Prosperity" was a nickname for Lao Gelin, but there was
no further elaboration of what exactly happened to the
Lao family. Afterward, Lao Mingchang uncovered faint
allusions to the 1909 accident in other places, yet they
were simple and seemed to have been written by insiders
who considered the subject taboo. This made the whole
business even more confusing. Lao Mingchang's theory
was that his grandfather had lost contact with the family
due to whatever occurred in 1909; but despite his great
interest, his research was stopped dead due to a lack of
detailed materials ... that is, until an unexpected event
in 2010 unearthed a new clue.

Due to his professional background in historical
and literary research, and because he often assisted
staff in the archives in book and document repair,
Lao Mingchang and his research work had always
been well known among Qingdao's history enthusi-
asts. When the Qingdao Municipal Institute of Cultural
Relics and Archaeology held an academic seminar in
the spring of 2010, it especially invited Lao to make
a report on the development of the business climate
in Qingdao during the period of German occupation.
It was during this meeting that Lao Mingchang met
Luo Guangsheng, a doctoral student from Qingdao
Ocean University. The broad knowledge of this young
man left a deep impression on Lao, and they became
fast friends of like mind.

At the time, Luo Guangsheng was engaged in the
study of folk religions, and so they mainly discussed the

secret School of Longevity. After reading through the materials collected by Luo Guangsheng, Lao Mingchang realized that the history of the School was perhaps much longer than he had first imagined. This was a secret society that had been circulating within the coastal areas of China for hundreds — or even thousands — of years. It possessed a vitality that greatly exceeded that of regular cults. During the Jin dynasty it was called the "Fushi Sect."[8] In the Tang dynasty it became the "Sect of the Golden Elixir." After the Mongols destroyed the southern Song dynasty and established the Yuan dynasty, the sect not only survived as a branch of shamanism but spread to the Korean peninsula. The so-called School of Longevity was just another name for its most recent incarnation. Although at first glance these secret societies did not appear to be connected, their doctrines of immortality were all surprisingly consistent. They believed that the gods created all living things from mud and water. Therefore, from the moment of conception, all beings resemble mud in that they have no fixed shape; but as they develop in the womb, they gradually adopt various forms. At the moment of birth the living creature no longer has any room to change, like a newly fired porcelain plate out of the kiln. Though the porcelain is hard, it cannot withstand any knocks. And just as the porcelain will break one day, so too must man and all other living things meet their death. Only by returning to one's roots, one's original appearance, can we repair our wounds as easily as mud changes shape, and obtain true longevity. Notably, these sects all spoke of

8    *Fushi* translates roughly to "drinking and eating."

something referred to as a "taisui" in the ancient books, and hinted that it was the key to immortality.

As bizarre and captivating as these stories were, what caught Lao's attention amidst the reams of documents was a small book recovered by Luo Guangsheng called *A Detailed Refutation of Falsehoods*. This work was written by a native of Jiaozhou named Wang Yupian[9] around the time of the late Qing dynasty and the early years of the Republic of China. In order to censor the spread of dangerous sects, this man personally investigated dozens of large and small cults circulating in the Shandong peninsula at the time — extracting and refuting their fallacies so that he could dissuade their followers. Naturally, the cults he investigated also included the School of Longevity, which had developed in the Jiaozhou Bay area. However, it was not the pamphlet's record of the School of Longevity that aroused Lao's interest, but a sentence written by Wang Yupian when refuting the heresies of the school.

> I heard that during August 1909, more than twenty people violently perished in the Qingdao residence of the Lao family. How can the School of Longevity not be evil?

This was the first time that Lao had ever seen any direct record of the calamity that befell the Lao family.

9    This fictional book and author are based on the real *A Detailed Refutation of Heresy*, written by Huang Yupian in 1838, which attacked local cults and superstitions of the time.

Although Wang Yupian stated that news of the Lao family had been on everybody's lips, there was no further evidence on the matter. Yet the period when the *Refutation* had been written, and the fact that Wang Yupian had lived in the Jiaozhou Bay area for over thirty years, made his statement more than credible. When Lao later told Luo Guangsheng about his discovery, the latter raised a very important point: it was impossible that the violent deaths of some twenty people in the Lao residence had escaped the attention of the relevant authorities. Even if locals had tried to deliberately conceal the news as some kind of self-imposed taboo, the archives of the colonial German government would inevitably have recorded it. If no such historical record existed in Qingdao it was likely that the relevant document had been taken away during the German departure of Qingdao. Lao Mingchang appreciated new possibilities in this idea. As it happened, 2010 coincided with the fifteenth anniversary of the official sister-city partnership between Qingdao and Mannheim, Germany. The two cities organized a series of exchanges to mark the occasion. Through some friends in the Qingdao Municipal Archives, Lao Mingchang managed to introduce his family history to several visiting members of the Mannheimer Altertumsverein in the hope that they could provide appropriate assistance. This move grasped the interest of several German scholars. Among them, Professor Haberger from Mannheim University's History Department immediately expressed his willingness to assist Lao Mingchang in his work by searching for the relevant historical documents in Germany.

This partnership came to fruition in the spring of

2011. In April of that year the Mannheimer Altertumsverein posted to Lao Mingchang copies of a 1909 report from the Qingdao police department, accompanied by other related files and translations into English. The registration date on the record was August 19; it had been filed by a German police officer by the name of Maximillian Adenauer. According to the case file, at the break of dawn several neighbors of the Lao family had gathered outside the patrol bureau's entrance in a state of extreme panic and unanimously demanded the police send a team to intervene at the residence. Officer Adenauer was on duty at the time, and with the help of the bureau's translator Song Hongxu he spent a considerable amount of time piecing together information from the stuttering residents before he comprehended what had happened. During the previous evening many loud noises had erupted from the courtyard of the Lao residence, including the crazed shouts and painful screams of many people, and the music of a shrill flute. Judging by the tumultuous uproar the courtyard must have been crowded with people, but no light appeared over the top of the wall. From afar, there was only darkness. This astonishing scene sparked terrible images in the imaginations of any onlookers. Neighbors shut windows and locked doors tight. None among them dared venture outside their home, let alone peek through the courtyard gate. The horrifying noise continued without abate in the blackness, and throughout not one light shone from the courtyard. Only with the rising of the morning sun did the cacophony subside. A few neighbors plucked up the courage to step outside, where they whiffed a noisome stench in the air, but still nobody dared approach the courtyard of the Lao family. Instead they ran to the police bureau once the situation seemed safe.

This was not the first time Officer Adenauer had heard rumors about Lao Gelin, so he rushed to the Lao residence immediately with Song Hongxu and some of the residents who hadn't been scared witless. An ominous sense of foreboding fell upon him when, arriving at the gate of the courtyard, he smelled the same odious fetor the neighbors had mentioned. He knocked on the door but nobody answered, so he gestured to one of his staff to kick the door down. With so many people at hand, they were through before long. The moment the great courtyard gate came crashing down the nauseating stench surged outward, and some even vomited. The two who had rushed to the front immediately lost consciousness. Others — including Officer Adenauer — felt their legs grow weak and fell back. Several turned and ran away. Those that remained refused to set foot within the courtyard and advised Officer Adenauer to do the same. Eventually, after acclimating himself to the scene in the courtyard and the suffocating stench, Officer Adenauer stepped carefully into the Lao residence alone. As he remembered it later, there were fifteen bodies lying scattered around the spacious courtyard, but the true terror was not their number — it was their condition. Each and every thoroughly rotten corpse had been reduced to bones and a pool of black mucus. The ubiquitous perturbing odor emanated from the turbid substance. After counting the bodies he ventured into the courtyard's three buildings and found a further thirteen corpses, in the same state as the ones outside: fetid messes of bones and noxious slime.

Separate reports stated that due to acute decomposition, officers could identify the deceased based on only their clothing or personal effects — which, strangely, did not carry the slightest hint of decay. The German authorities calculated that twenty-two of the deceased were Lao Gelin and his family members, while the remaining six were servants. This meant that except for the child Lao Siwei, who had been sent to the northeast one year previously, this accident had eradicated the entire Lao family. The majority of the corpses — or what was left of them — showed no signs of struggle. A German medical officer analyzed some of the black mucus to little effect.

In July and August, the Mannheimer Altertumsverein sent several photocopies detailing how the colonial administration had followed up on the incident. Governor Alfred Meyer-Waldeck ordered a strict blockade on any news regarding the situation and a thorough clean-up of the Lao residence to avoid causing greater panic. Later, during the latter half of 1910, ownership of the courtyard was transferred for a low price to a German businessman named William Heisenberg, who had recently arrived in Qingdao. Heisenberg also mysteriously disappeared within three months of residing at the compound. Prior to his disappearance, he claimed to have found something very unusual inside the house, and at the same time had complained that there was often a peculiar odor in the courtyard that was accompanied at night by harsh whistling and the sound of many people babbling. This incident caused those nearly forgotten superstitions to flourish once again. Hence, the governor's office resorted to hiring two priests to conduct an exorcism within the courtyard, before ordering its permanent closure. From that moment onward there is no further information regarding the Lao family.

Though these documents did not satisfyingly conclude the calamity that had befallen the Lao family, at least they resolved some of the doubts that Lao Mingchang had held, leaving him quite encouraged. As a researcher with more than twenty years' experience at the Cultural Relics and Archaeology Institute, he understood that his knowledge of historical events would always have a number of blank spaces and mysteries. Indeed, this was one of the charms of historical research. Even so, these reports did bring him one surprise. His previous materials had all been vague about the exact address of the Lao residence, but the case files sent from Germany clearly stated the street and house number of where the building had been situated. The prospect of finding his ancestral home greatly excited Lao. After studying the maps of Qingdao during the German occupation in fine detail alongside Luo Guangsheng, Lao Mingchang was finally able to determine the exact location of the Lao family's residence — in fact, it was not far at all from his apartment on Xiao Yushan.

## 4.

Following adequate preparation, Lao and Luo stepped out one afternoon in November 2011 to search for the site of the former Lao residence. They took with them the official administrative map of Qingdao alongside an old map from the German occupation period for comparison, as well as a camera and notebook to record any possible discoveries. The two men followed Yushan Road down to Xiao Yushan, passing by the Qingdao Museum of History and Culture, before entering University Road on the left with its sycamore trees on both sides. Since it was already the beginning of winter more than half of the sycamore leaves had fallen off, leaving a clear view of the twisted lychee tree branches stretching grotesquely into the sky. On one side of University Road was the high red wall adorned with glazed yellow tiles of the museum and art gallery; and on the other side was a cast-iron fence built onto a grey granite base. Behind the fence were the remains of a small European-style enclosure left over from the periods of German and Japanese occupation. There were two double-storied buildings in the enclosure: they were built in different styles and had both been eroded by time, though the buildings retained an air of faded grandeur. The neglected enclosure was cluttered with an assortment of dull old objects; clusters of yellowing weeds peeped out of the gaps between the junk. All of this added a sorrowful tone that intertwined with the overarching sense of nostalgia.

Before long, the pair lost their way due to the many adjustments made to the municipal plans and the numerous alleyways that were unmarked on the map. Yet Lao remained untroubled. Walking through the winding alleys gave him the impression that he had left modern, prosperous Qingdao and returned to the world that had existed a century before. Once or twice he recognized some landmarks that he had read about in historical materials, such as the dried-up bed of the Qingdao River or a building from a hundred years ago. The cement road underfoot would occasionally morph into rugged old cobbled lanes, and several courtyard doors were covered in rust stains. Even buildings erected in the 1980s and 1990s seemed worn and quaint. Then, after some time, he spotted a two-story building built in the German style. It was an elegant, if overly conspicuous, building with a steep brick-red folding roof and narrow windows embedded between delicate arches. The greyish-yellow gable facing the street was aged, and the decorative arches and round pedestal columns were crumbling apart. Between the building and the wall along the street was a tall tree that had lost all its leaves, but its thick branches still obstructed one of the small building's corners. Lao would later recall in his diary an overwhelming feeling of déjà vu. His mind was made up: after comparing the two maps in his hand, this had to be the residence of the Lao family, or at least a portion of it. Now it had a new name — Number 5 Longkou Road.

The site of the Lao family had lost its original appearance completely through the passing of the years. The extraordinarily tall walls that were often mentioned in the historical texts had long been demolished and supplanted by simple brick walls built by nearby residents. The two supplementary wings were also long gone, leaving only the main building preserved. Today, one of those low dormitory-style structures that had commonly been built in the 1970s and 1980s accompanied the old main building. A row of bicycles and electric scooters used by the residents were parked in the wide-open space between the two buildings, while the bases of the walls away from the main intersection were stacked with everyday utensils and pots or broken basins for growing vegetables and flowers. From the outside looking in, all of these little scenes brought a sense of nostalgia to the aspects of life in the courtyard. Yet strangely, every object had been deliberately placed some distance away from the old building, which was left alone in its own empty corner, almost as though it existed independently from its surroundings.

Restraining his excitement, Lao walked into the court-yard hoping for a closer look, but discovered nobody lived within the old building and that the windows were covered in layers of grey dust. However, the granite bases of the walls, the carved plaques almost wiped clean by time, the dilapidated stone carvings and railings ... all of these allowed onlookers to peek through the decay at the luxury and comfort of yesteryear. Hence, the pair turned to other areas and found an old man sunbathing in the courtyard to talk with.

The old man was called Li Rongde, a native of Qingdao. He told Lao and Luo that the owner of the old building lived outside of town and returned only one or two weeks a year to clean the interior up slightly. He never stayed overnight inside the house, and the house was always empty. Years ago a series of people attempted to rent the old building; and in each case they had always found another place to stay after a couple of months. The strange smells that would occasionally emanate from an unknown location in the house led the neighbors to be ill-disposed toward it. There were also rumors that the house was haunted. Some said they could hear the faint sound of voices coming from certain areas close to the building, though never clearly enough to be intelligible.

Others spoke of a music coming from inside. Li Rongde added at length that these stories were not to be taken too seriously. He had lived in the courtyard for over twenty years and heard many of the old wives' tales, but nobody really had any proof of goings-on. It was true there was a strange odor, as he had smelled it often himself — in all probability a problem with the drains and nothing out of the ordinary.

As for Lao Mingchang, these bizarre rumors were nothing more than unpredicted interludes on the route to discovery. The sight of the place where his ancestors once lived was enough to satisfy him, and the situation related to the building gave him some new ideas. One month after he learned of the old building, he contacted the owner of the house, and after relating the whole story he eventually negotiated to rent it as his new home for a relatively low price. According to Lao's diary, the interior was in a poor condition due to it being unoccupied for many years. The partition walls had all suffered damage, and some of the wooden floors on the second floor needed to be replaced completely. In actual fact the entire building was barely anything but an outer shell. Yet Lao harbored no complaints, and instead hired some people to thoroughly clean out and renovate the old thing. This was an unimaginable course of action in the eyes of the neighbors, but the support of Luo Guangsheng and the characteristic stubbornness of the elderly caused him to persist in his efforts. After all, this was the site where his ancestors had lived a hundred years ago; the excitement this roused within Lao Mingchang is easy to imagine.

The renovation work continued until late March 2012,

and Lao moved into the house in early April to begin his new life. Those early days in the old building were not particularly comfortable, judging from his diary entries from that time. Though the house had been remodeled and refurbished, the water pressure and electricity were far less stable than those found in modern buildings. During the winter of 2012 he also encountered the problem of insufficient heating. However, aside from the inconvenience caused by these early renovations, what really confused him was the disgusting smell mentioned by the neighbors. He described it in his diary as something akin to the smell found in an animal after it dies and begins to decompose. More troubling for Lao was his inability to find its source. The scent was most noticeable in a small windowless room on the east side of the ground floor, and markedly fainter once outside of the room, when it could be detected only occasionally; on the first floor there was hardly any trace of it at all. Yet there were times when the smell turned especially pungent and made its presence known even up on the first floor or outside the house. The room, however, was empty: barely a space of two hundred feet contained between four brick walls. The cemented floor of the room had been installed during a renovation several decades previously when the decaying wooden floorboards had been replaced, so it was unlikely that it concealed some kind of dead animal. Not only that, but before he had moved in, the house had been uninhabited for more than a decade. If somebody had buried something, then by now it would have rotted away completely; furthermore, complaints regarding strange smells had accompanied the house throughout its entire history. As far back as the beginning of the twentieth century, the former German merchant William Heisenberg — who had been the final occupant of the Lao residence before its closure by the colonial governor — had complained about the stench prior to his mysterious disappearance.

The strange smell may have been nothing other than unpleasant distraction, but another more ominous mystery had begun to make its presence felt. Lao Mingchang noticed this mystery for the first time one month after moving in. He wrote every detail from that period into his diary. On the afternoon of May 9, 2012, Lao had felt tired after dinner, switched off the television, and lay down on the sofa in the ground floor living room. When the time arrived for him to open his eyes, the sky had darkened utterly; the only light a small ray slipping in from the streetlight. The time must have been late indeed; there was not a peep from any direction. He still lay half-asleep on the sofa, waiting for full wakefulness, when he suddenly thought that he heard some vague, faint rustling. At first he thought they were only the remnant of a dream and that he was not yet fully awake, so he ignored them and lay motionless. Some time passed, yet still the sound persisted — never truly distinct, always on the cusp of audibility. He was certain it wasn't a mouse or some other such animal but was in fact a person speaking. The voice, however, was too weak for the content to be distinguished. He wanted to get up, to go see, but petrifying tension had frozen his body in place; he was completely unable to move. The muffled echoes continued in this way for ten to fifteen minutes then gradually faded away from the edge of earshot. Once gone, it took a few minutes for Lao to slowly pry himself from the sofa at last. There in the darkness he stood for some time before turning on the light and giving the house a thorough inspection. All doors and windows were locked; there was no sign of destruction, and no indication that any other person had entered the house, except for the omnipresent stench, more violently obvious now than he had ever encountered. Lao later admitted in his diary that it might have been merely an illusion caused by nerves.

Yet this was only the beginning. In August Lao heard the sounds a further three times, each time feeling that they were growing increasingly regular. He suspected that this might be because they were too indistinct and were perhaps trying not to attract attention. The last three occurrences had all taken place deep in the night, though maybe that was the only time sufficiently quiet to make out the faint resonances. Each occurrence lasted approximately five to fifteen minutes. Just like the first time, it appeared to be the voices of people speaking, but as before they were too vague to comprehend. On one occasion he also heard something like an oddly cadenced whistle or flute; only slightly more noticeable than the human voices. Whenever the noise vanished he would inspect all doors and windows in the house, finding nothing each time. The third time he heard the sounds — by which I mean the time he heard the whistle — he steeled his resolve and carefully searched around the house for their source, eventually realizing the voices seemingly emanated from the small room on the eastern side of the ground floor where the stench was most powerful. However, there was nothing in the room that could have created such a noise: in actual fact, he hadn't placed anything in the room at all. After the fourth time, he finally made up his mind to find a reasonable explanation at all costs — this eerie mystery was starting to shatter his nerves.

No doubt the small, suspicious room was the obvious starting point; but his initial inspections failed to reveal anything of value, until a simple measurement revealed the room's secret. According to the layout of the house, the mysterious little room should have been rectangular, yet the one before him was more of a square. Perhaps a hidden mezzanine behind the room's eastern wall? He called Luo Guangsheng over to help him scrape off the plaster from the eastern wall, confirming his suspicions: there was a sealed door beneath the mortar. The material used to seal the door was a very old-fashioned type of German brickwork, which narrowed the likely perpetrators down to three — either the door had been sealed by a member of the Lao family, the foreign merchant William Heisenberg, or the German authorities when they had ordered the closure of the courtyard. Whomever had sealed it, the message they had wished to convey was clear. Not only had they totally sealed off the door, they had also deliberately scratched the plaster off the entire wall and re-painted it, thus hiding the door within the partition wall without leaving a trace of their handiwork. The amount of effort poured into the task clearly indicated the perpetrator not only wished to prevent anyone else from entering the mezzanine; they had also wanted to bury the secret behind the door for good, where no one would ever rediscover it. Perversely, this form of concealment imbued in the men an even greater desire to open it. Needless to say, it was more than likely that the mezzanine behind the door contained further clues related to the ancestors of the Lao family. So it was that on August 29 — two days after the discovery of the hidden door — they hired a laborer to open the sealed portal.

The instant the laborer breached the door, all three men smelled that the fetid odor was now worse than ever, so they paused and waited for the smell to disperse before clearing the remaining bricks. The narrow mezzanine had enough room for only two people to enter side by side. The wooden floorboards had mostly rotted away, and were smothered thickly with dust and debris. At the end of the mezzanine was a square hole in the ground covered by a broken trapdoor ... the death-smell was coming from that hole. An ancient lock hung from the trapdoor, rusted to such a degree that it was impossible to make out its original appearance. Lao called upon the laborer to break open the lock.

The trapdoor was pulled open revealing a cave underneath. It was about a dozen feet to the ground below. The opening bordered one of the walls of the cellar; but there was no ladder, and the constrained space prevented observation of what lurked at the bottom of the cellar. Since they lacked the necessary tools, they had no choice other than to close the trapdoor and plan to return once better prepared.

## 5.

One week passed before they opened the trapdoor again. Judging from the contents of his diary, Lao Mingchang had some concerns about entering the cellar and investigating further. It wasn't fear of ghosts, demons, or any other fairy tale that stopped him, but fear of actual danger. Considering that his ancestors had been suspected of smuggling, it was more than possible that secret passages existed under the house for conducting underground business. The voices from the room likely belonged to people using these old secret tunnels to carry out certain activities. Although he did not know what these people were up to, it was clear that he had better not rush into finding the source of those voices without a comprehension of the situation at hand. For security purposes, Lao also installed a new lock on the trapdoor the same day the cellar was discovered, and hired someone to fit a much sturdier door. By contrast, the younger Luo could not contain his enthusiasm for the mysterious basement. Not only did he make arrangements for the equipment and tools needed for underground exploration, but he also eventually persuaded Lao to enter the cellar with him.

At noon on September 8, Lao and Luo opened the trapdoor, attached a rope ladder, and descended into the aperture with their equipment. They were so well prepared — their gear included a carbon dioxide detector — that when the two men actually crossed the threshold they found the exploration to be far less difficult than imagined. They experienced no breathing difficulties despite the air being full of that somehow-familiar pungency, and the carbon dioxide readings were safe. Still, their surroundings surprised them more than a little.

Beneath the opening was an arched tunnel made of brick. The passage was more than ten feet wide and equally high. A series of ingenious archways were placed at varying distances to provide structural support. The brickwork of the walls had also been arranged precisely; there were even recesses for oil lamps. On one side of the passageway — the side opposite the aperture — a large lacquered gate sat within an alcove. The door panel was recessed about three feet inward from the tunnel walls, leaving a shallow empty space as a porch. There was no need for a canopy over the gate since it was underground; but the steps in front of it, the pillars beside it, and the four *menzan*[10] above it were exactly the same. The door panels were dilapidated; one had already broken from its hinges and collapsed to the ground. The other had crumbled so far one was afraid to even touch it. Two plaques hung on either side of the doorway. Upon the right was written "A Thousand Branches from One Seed," and on the left was "Ten Thousand Brethren from One Root." In the middle, above the door, was another plaque: "Ancestral Hall of the Lao Family." The chiseled lettering still retained some remains of paint, though it was already impossible to determine what the original color had been.

Lao was shocked by this revelation. As a place to worship one's ancestors and conduct major ceremonies, the chosen location of an ancestral temple naturally attaches

10   *Menzan* are small hexagonal wooden studs placed over a doorway to denote the occupant's wealth and status during traditional times. Two *menzan* would represent the house of a common person; four *menzan* would mean the house belongs to a well-established person like a wealthy merchant or an official.

great importance to its fengshui and the convenience of traveling to it — but building one's ancestral temple beneath one's own family courtyard was singularly rare behavior, if not outright deviancy. He was reminded of the letters he had read during his research that claimed the Lao family had excavated tons of earth during the construction of their home. Why had his own ancestors been so secretive about their ancestral temple? The two men did not linger before the gate overlong; after some cursory glances they instead entered the temple from the half-collapsed doorway. Behind the door stretched a spacious rectangular room that roughly corresponded to the specifications of a courtyard within a normal ancestral hall. There were no objects displayed in the corridor, but there were words engraved upon the walls to the left and right. The words on the right were a concise account of the migration of the Lao family from Yanguan in Zhejiang Province to Jimo in Shandong Province and then to Qingdao. The words on the left described the process of Lao Gelin's construction of the family temple for the honor of his ancestors. The writing on the wall was nothing unfamiliar to Lao Mingchang, so he did not pay any special attention to it. At the end of the room there was yet another lacquered gate identical in style to the previous one; however, this gate was in relatively good condition and lacked any plaques above or beside it.

After carefully pushing open the door an almost square room was revealed on the other side and yet another open doorway on the opposite wall. According to the spatial layout this place should have corresponded to the ancestral temple room used to perform sacrifices to the ancestors. The required table for the arrangement of ancestral tablets during the ritual, however, was absent. The whole room was empty, with only a shallow sunken pit in the center. The pit was over ten feet in diameter, one foot in depth, with a curved inner wall that had been polished so smoothly that it resembled a large pot embedded in the ground. Surrounding the pit were a handful of fully decayed straw mats. These must have been used for worship during the sacrifices, though Lao Mingchang was unable to imagine what kind of sacrifices may have been performed. Strange murals depicting what appeared to be acts of worship covered every wall, but the paint had peeled in most places, leaving the image of something resembling a bulbous black boulder. Aside from the most conspicuous objects, the only things in the room were four oil lamps placed at great height in the corners of the room and some waist-high wooden boxes leaning against a wall. The boxes were not well preserved. Donning a pair of gloves, Lao Mingchang carefully opened a box and found that it was filled with ancient books, in even worse condition than the box itself. They were shrouded within piles of ash formed by the decay of paper — in a state of near total deterioration — disintegrated beyond recognition. By the glow of the flashlight he was able to identify a few books in somewhat better condition, but he saw that most of them were what was commonly accepted as pseudepigrapha, apocrypha, or other collections of outlandish tales. There were one or two handwritten manuscripts of the *Kunlun Scriptures*, which legend said were part of *The Classic of Mountains and Seas* but which had never been recognized within academic circles. There was also a bound copy of the *Records of Universal Harmony*[11] dating from the Ming dynasty and a printed version of the *Records of the Great Wilderness* produced in the Qing dynasty. Presumably these were the ancient books that Lao Gelin spent so much capital to collect from across the globe. There were three more books in the boxes — tightly packaged in oiled paper — in addition to the fragmented old tomes. These were in much better condition due to the protection from the oiled paper. Lao took one of them from the boxes, shook off the dust, and after carefully opening it discovered that inside was page after page of unbound manuscript with Lao Gelin's name on the letterhead. He handed the three packages to Luo for later study.

Having investigated the room, they passed through the doorway opposite and entered another corridor, identical to the one they had passed through previously, except its walls were covered in the remarkable achievements of the Lao family's ancestors. At this point Lao was able to estimate the rough layout of the entire subterranean compound. Going by the traditional three-tiered structure of an ancestral temple, the deepest part of the building at the end of this corridor should be a hall used to house the ancestral tablets. This roused an unspeakable tension and excitement within him when he pushed open the final lacquered gate. What lay beyond this portal would be his reward for a lifelong study of his family's history — witnessing his ancestors, not as a researcher but as a descendant.

11    A collection of myths, legends, and tall tales dating from the Tang dynasty (618–907).

The flashlight illuminated a room the size of a Hall of Offerings. Both men looked around and gasped — a staircase made of sturdy earth and slate rose out of every other side of the room. The outermost level was waist-high, extending step-by-step upward until they almost reached the ceiling of the cellar. Together they formed an enormous semicircle. Later, when Lao and Luo had the chance to discuss this scene in detail, Luo suggested that the steps resembled the seats of a huge auditorium. From a certain grotesque point of view, this was a horrifying allusion — for placed upon each of the steps were the hallowed ancestral tablets, in neat rows like the scales on a fish. Though some of the tablets had collapsed, the majority of them remained in their original position. The light from the torch cast long and weird flickering shadows from the tablets buried beneath thick layers of dust, evoking the unmistakable aura of tombstones in a benighted graveyard. Their number obliterated Lao's expectations and strained his imagination — there must have been 1,500 to 2,000 tablets, each of them representing an ancestor of the family. Lao was at a loss as to how his great-grandfather knew the names of all these ancestors, but in such a dark atmosphere this ghoulish display cast inexplicable dread upon him. After three years of research and investigation, he was familiar only with the names of fewer than one hundred of his ancestors. Here within this morbid ancestral temple that number would fill a small corner at most; the vast majority of names were complete strangers to him. He would later recall in his diary that an oppressive, suffocating atmosphere almost crushed him to the ground, and he dared not take another step. Yet even now, intense curiosity and enthusiasm to learn more about his family history drove him to continue. So he bowed to the ancestral tablets arrayed on the three sides around him and then stepped forward to take a closer look.

This revealed a more subtle, but just as extraordinary, detail. Upon closer examination of the decayed and colorless tablets, Lao discovered that although the names and ranks of family seniority written thereupon genuinely corresponded to the ancestry of the family, the tablets themselves were not in fact the correct tablets for the worship of the dead. These tablets were used for worshipping living people who were praying for long life, even for those ancestors who according to their position in the family lineage should have lived hundreds or thousands of years ago. This violation of common sense sent Lao into a deep state of confusion. Were his great-grandfather and other relatives so obsessed with the idea of immortality that they refused to believe that their ancestors had already passed away, expending all their energy on this form of bizarre self-hypnosis? Following this train of thought, Lao began to pity his ancestors. For there among the rows of longevity tablets he saw his own great-great-grandfather — Lao Gelin's father, Lao Xiuwen — and remembered how he had already died just one year prior to the family's move from Jimo to Qingdao in 1897.

Lao and Luo left the unnerving subterranean hall with more questions than ever but stopped during their departure to check once more the tunnel in front of the temple. This passageway confirmed some of Lao's assumptions, because one end of it connected to an abandoned corner of a sewer system built during the German occupation period. The other end sloped gently downward, passed through several bends, and finally connected to an underground cave leading to the sea. The cave seemed to be a granite fissure formed by nature. When Lao and Luo arrived at the cave, the tide was already beginning to rise. Before them was a long black muddy tidal flat that was repeatedly bashed by dark waters pounding against it. The characteristic fishy scent of the sea was faintly tinged with the ever-present noxiousness. The far end of the cave was already submerged with water; Lao, however, was sure that the ebbing tide would reveal a hidden cave leading to Qingdao's waterfront. The Lao family must have used this tunnel during those years to bypass the eyes and ears of others in order to carry out their smuggling business or other furtive seafaring in secret. As for how they had discovered this natural estuary, it was difficult for Lao Mingchang to guess.

The exploration answered many of Lao Mingchang's questions. The stench that infiltrated his house must have emanated from the old German sewer network, and the eerie sounds he could hear were definitive proof that some people still used the ancient underground passages to engage in secret activities. Lao Mingchang began to worry about his household security, so he strengthened the trapdoor leading down to the passageways and locked the small room. The biggest surprise of the expedition, however, was the three bundles wrapped in oiled paper they had retrieved from the underground family temple.

# 6.

The three bundles had been packaged with a simple moisture-proof method and were not prepared for long-term preservation. Hence, the manuscripts contained within the packages were inadequately preserved and in need of considerable careful repair. The inscriptions upon the pages and their content left no doubt that they were the work of his great-grandfather Lao Gelin. One half of the manuscripts were notes left behind by Lao Gelin from his studies of those ancient decaying books found within the boxes; the other half seemed to be records of conversations Lao Gelin had conducted with a variety of different types of people. Some of the recorded dialogues were extremely simple; nothing more than a series of questions and answers on certain days of certain months. Others were much more detailed and included not only the causes and effects behind these questions and answers but also Lao Gelin's commentary and textual criticism. The topics of these conversations covered a broad range: some seemed to be related to the content of the ancient books, some were preposterously outlandish stories, and quite a number involved the history and secrets of the longevity sect. The most confusing part of these conversations, however, was not the actual topics of discussion but the people Lao Gelin was holding them with. These people included a large number of the Lao family's ancestors as well as many other people seemingly unconnected to the family. No matter who they were, they all shared one peculiar characteristic: they had all lived in times much older than Lao Gelin's own. There were several sections of the manuscripts that recounted the time when Lao Gelin had conversed with an imperial censor from the early years of the Ming dynasty called Sun Mu about a legendary star known as "Yuggoth." It was said to be a dark unshining star that orbited beyond the known solar system[12] invisible to the naked eye of mere mortals. Other pages recorded a conversation Lao You — an ancestor of the Lao family — had conducted with a hermit named "Hsan the Greater" during the time of the Eastern Han dynasty.[13]

This bizarre content left Lao Mingchang utterly confounded. These letters were undoubtedly strange stories or odd rumors heard by his great-grandfather Lao Gelin and retold in the form of a question-and-answer session. Given the famed profound depth of knowledge possessed by the Lao family this would not have been difficult. Yet it was the motive behind his great-grandfather's collection of stories that left him truly perplexed. Perhaps they were used as proof of the claims toward immortality and distributed among the believers. After all, many of the ancestors of the Lao family maintained that those who had already achieved immortality had taught their esoteric knowledge to them. However, the manuscripts were not only too casual and fragmented

12   The known solar system of the time would have extended only to Saturn, meaning that Pluto — a.k.a. Yuggoth — would have been unknown.

13   "Hsan the Greater" is the author of *The Seven Cryptical Books of Hsan*, mentioned in Lovecraft's "The Other Gods" and *The Dream-Quest of Unknown Kadath*.

but were mixed with notes of suspicious origin and devoid of rhyme or reason, indicating that they were not meant for public consumption. On the other hand, the dialogues appeared to conceal deeper truths that were meaningful only to those readers with the required background knowledge.

Amidst all of these conversational stories the ones that most fascinated Lao were several dialogues between Lao Gelin and a man named Lao Fu — he even wrote in his diary about the intention of his great-grandfather in writing this tale. Lao recognized the name of "Lao Fu" because it was none other than the name of the ancestor given the most prominent and honored position in the subterranean ancestral temple — the first ancestor and progenitor of the entire Lao family. This "dialogue" between his great-grandfather and his first ancestor was a myth-building exercise in revealing the origins of the Lao family and those of the longevity sect.

Within this discussion, Lao Fu claimed to have studied sorcery from an alchemist when he was young. Later, following the recommendation of others, he became an official at the imperial court and gained the trust of the emperor. One day, the emperor asked him how he could prolong his life and he told the emperor about the Fairy Mountains[14] and immortals recorded in the ancient books. The emperor was overjoyed when he heard this and ordered Lao Fu to find the secluded immortals and seek out the elixir of immortality. Lao Fu persisted in this mission for eight years without success. Later, during

14   In Chinese legend, the Fairy Mountains are islands to the east of China and are the abode of the immortals.

a sea voyage in search of the Fairy Mountains, his fleet was hit by a storm and was blown toward a deserted island. The ship was badly damaged and unable to sail further, so Lao Fu could only order his men to repair the ship while he led a handful of disciples to the island to seek supplies.

Half a day later a group of disciples brought back something very peculiar. The thing was the size of a jar, dark and smooth, with no mouth, eyes, or appendages. It felt like meat but was much softer. But the most astonishing thing was that when a disciple used a knife to cut a piece from it, there was no blood to be seen, and the incision shortly grew back to its original shape perfectly intact. Lao Fu asked his disciples where they had found the thing, to which they replied, "In a shallow bay." They also said there were many others like it in the water — some large, some small — being pecked upon by seabirds. As to what it was nobody knew, so they brought one back. Lao Fu took a closer look and suddenly remembered a passage contained within one of the ancient books that mentioned a kind of strange creature known as a "taisui," allegedly very similar to the thing in front of him. The books said that the taisui was endless, capable of replicating itself, and once eaten allowed one to shed one's mortal body and be reborn. So he cut a piece from the thing and ate it, only to discover that it was tasteless. When his disciples saw that it was safe to eat, they also divided the thing and devoured it.

It took them another ten days to repair the ship. Lao Fu worried about the taisui; though he visited the shallow bay every day, he never saw it. On the day they set sail Lao Fu once again visited the shallow bay alone but as before found nothing. When he returned to the ship, he discovered that the entire entourage of over a dozen sailors and disciples had disappeared. There was nobody on the boat; though the food, potable water, and daily clothing were suspiciously untouched and in their original positions. He cried out to them at the top of his voice and heard a chattering of human voices coming from the water at the side of the boat, so he poked his head out to take a look. But there were no humans in the water — there was an abomination. Its whole body was smooth and black; it had neither head or tail: a bubbling mass of chaos with hundreds of eyes across its body staring in all directions and hundreds of mouths speaking in a thousand tongues. The monster's countless mouths babbled ceaselessly, shouting, hooting, screaming! When it espied Lao Fu it sprang violently onto the ship's side, scrabbling and spilling onto the boat like a mudslide. The ship was small and narrow — Lao Fu had nowhere to flee. He could only kneel and beg for mercy. Strange as it is to say, the monster brought him no harm. Instead, its unhinging mouths spoke like thousands of people in unison.

The monster told Lao Fu there was no need to be afraid. He had eaten its flesh, which bestowed upon those who consumed it the power to shed one's mortal body. The other sailors had already become immortals and crossed the seas to live among the Fairy Mountains, and now it had come to deliver Lao Fu there as well. Feeling suspicious, Lao Fu asked the monster exactly what kind of creature it was. The monster replied that it was the creation of the Amphiura Gods;[15] at the maw of chaos' first yawning, when heaven and earth first began to form, the Elder Amphiura descended from the stars to this mortal world. When the Gods saw that the earth was devoid of life, they crafted the taisui from soil and water, then took a piece from it to create all the living things in the world — thus, the taisui was the ancestor of all life. Upon hearing this Lao Fu quickly prostrated himself and worshipped the creature, asking of it where the Amphiura Gods were now. The monster replied the Amphiura Gods had departed for the austral reaches of the world where no living being could enter and hadn't been seen for hundreds of thousands of years. Now in turn the monster questioned Lao Fu: why did he seek the Amphiura Gods? Lao Fu explained about the emperor's order to find the elixir of immortality, reasoning that if the Amphiura Gods had created all the living things in the world then they must also have some means by which mortals could live forever. At this, the monster's hundreds of horrible mouths gaped and choked out a hooting sound that may have been laughter, and it replied that when the Amphiura Gods took the living creatures of the world from its flesh their shape had become fixed. Fish were fish, birds were birds, and men were men. And since the bodies of living creatures could be damaged, they could not be replaced. In the long run even the sturdiest of statues will one day be smashed. That of the flesh must

15  Amphiura is a large genus of brittle starfish found in oceans worldwide, but especially in the Arctic and Antarctica. As to what they represent in this story, the reader can draw their own conclusions.

ultimately die. If one wished to become immortal, it said, one must cast off one's flesh and body and return to the fountainhead of life. Only then could one undergo thousands of transformations to live forever and ever.

Lao Fu beseeched the monster to grant him the secrets of immortality. It replied that in ancient times there was the country of Great Peng,[16] whose ruler was on familiar terms with the creature. It had given the monarch its flesh to eat, and the monarch had lived for eight hundred years. Eventually Great Peng was destroyed by the state of Chu, and the monarch, full of disheartenment, had gone with the monster to live in the Fairy Mountains across the sea. Lao Fu had once read the story of Great Peng, but was not so acquainted with the exact details, so the monster summoned the ruler of Great Peng and introduced them to one another. Lao Fu inquired upon some of the details described in the ancient books, which the monarch confirmed were correct. From this moment onward, Lao Fu believed. He begged the monster to share the secrets of immortality in order to restore the emperor's life. Seeing his determination, the monster began to drag the boat and ferry Lao Fu across the sea, back to the mainland, and offered him a portion of his flesh to take with him. The monster gave a warning to Lao Fu before it departed. It said, although it permitted Lao Fu to offer its flesh to the emperor, the day would come when it would return to the one who consumed it and carry them away to the Fairy Mountains across the sea. And if the passenger refused the monster's

16   Great Peng was a Chinese Bronze Age state in what is now Jiangsu Province.

claim, not even immortality would save them. Lao Fu must always remember to come to the sea to find it. Having spoken these words, the monster sank beneath the ocean. Lao Fu bowed his gratitude and gathered his piece of the taisui, and rushed to the capital through day and night. Yet before he had even completed half of the journey, news came that the emperor had already passed away. The succeeding emperor blamed his predecessor's death upon the sorcerer who had once lobbied within the imperial court, and pursued the culprit with all his might. In desperation, Lao Fu could gather his family only in secret, change his name, and flee. Such was the origin of the Lao family and the longevity cult.[17]

After careful examination of the manuscripts, Lao Mingchang concluded that those ancient books had overly influenced his great-grandfather when he had written this strange story. Parts of the manuscript that

17  Those familiar with Chinese history may have noticed the similarity between Lao Fu and the historical figure of Xu Fu. Born in 255 BC before the advent of the Qin dynasty, he served as a court sorcerer and was sent by the first emperor of China to seek the elixir of immortality across the eastern sea. After a second voyage in 210 BC he never returned. Some say he landed in Japan, where he is still revered under the name of Jofuku. Other legends say that Xu Fu began his voyage from Mount Lao (Lao Shan), near Qingdao. The character "Lao" in Lao Shan is almost the same as the character used for the Lao family in this story, which was also the name used by the descendants of Xu Fu, who never followed him to sea but stayed in the Lao Shan area instead.

highlighted the portions of the research gathered there also made frequent mention of a similar creature to the one described in the story. Those antediluvian times referred to it as a "taisui," "legion," or "the all-seeing flesh." Though the name underwent countless changes, its depiction remained more or less the same. Esoteric scrolls described the thing as something created by the elder gods from earth and water, and a number of the ancient works agreed that the gods had used it as the basis of all life. Other books regarded it as the epitome of achievement since all creatures in heaven and earth had emerged from its body. Almost all the records claimed that the thing was immortal and capable of self-rejuvenation even if cut apart; more asserted that devouring its flesh could allow one to ascend to immortal perfection.

These legends naturally presented a great temptation to the immortality-obsessed members of the Lao family, and so it was obvious to Lao Mingchang why his great-grandfather would have made up such a story. It also explained why the tablets placed within the Lao ancestral temple had been used to craft those bizarre dialogues: since the stories claimed that the Lao family had grasped the secrets of immortality and their ancestors had never died a mortal death but had only followed the monster across the sea to the Fairy Mountains. From a modern perspective, however, this was nothing more than mere superstition and fantasy resulting from the wishful thinking of his ancestors. The Lao family could never have believed that their lineage would ultimately end in such an abrupt and violent manner despite all their self-hypnosis and delusion. Only the youngest son who had left his hometown survived the great calamity that befell the Lao family; only he could continue the family line. As Lao Mingchang expected, the young Luo Guangsheng was fascinated by the entire account. He even told Lao that the story written in the manuscript was most likely true — or at least partly true. Many historical documents clearly proved that the secret longevity cult had been circulating the legend of the taisui long before the time of Lao Gelin. More importantly, Luo claimed that he had seen the taisui personally.

# 7.

Looking back, it is difficult for us to speculate on the impact Luo Guangsheng's opinions had on Lao Mingchang. What is certain is that in November 2012 — two months after they found the manuscript — Lao accepted Luo's invitation to participate in a weird gathering, and saw with his own eyes the taisui so often mentioned in his great-grandfather's documents. Before departing for the meeting, Luo had told him that the people at the gathering all had a deep understanding of the secret teachings of longevity, even the taisui itself — and furthermore, had divined a means of locating it.

There were ten people at the gathering and all of them appeared very friendly, especially after Luo introduced Lao's family background to them. The revelation of his heritage brought a respectful tone to their words that left the simple-living Lao feeling both happy and proud. With great enthusiasm they invited him to introduce his research on his family history and the School of Longevity, raising a great many questions in regards to some of the details. Naturally, they also allowed Lao to observe the taisui they had found in return. It was a black object about the size of a cooking pot submerged in water, but with a form closer to a sphere: completely smooth on its surface, with no protrusions, visible organs, or limbs. It was similar to what had been described in the ancient books and the manuscripts of Lao Gelin. Whenever somebody would reach out a hand to grab it, Lao noticed that the thing seemed to be very soft — more like a semi-flowing viscous substance — and that it changed shape under the influence of any external pressure. Upon closer inspection, the surface of the taisui appeared to be somewhat transparent, with the faint trace of seemingly animate objects undulating beneath it. Whatever the thing was, it was certainly not animal, because Lao was unable to detect any kind of reaction whatsoever to external stimuli. One of the participants told him that it was an extremely old mycobacterial complex — a collection of protoplasm. In fact, there were many records of such organisms within ancient Chinese books, where it was believed they contained the power to extend one's years and to even bestow immortality. The participant further explained that this obviously didn't mean that the thing could transform people into immortals, but it was undeniable that there were still many unsolved mysteries within modern science and so it was unreasonable to dismiss the collective experience of the ancients completely.

Whether it was the friendliness and respect shown by the group that moved him, or the mysterious taisui, regarded so highly by his ancestors, and the longevity cult that evoked his interest, Lao accepted the invitation to participate in several more gatherings over the following two months, where he acquainted himself with a new circle of friends. The main topic of conversation at these gatherings was the various descriptions of the taisui that could be found in diverse arcane books, myths, and legends, so the strange stories and research notes written by Lao's great-grandfather were quickly circulated. Some of the activities at these gatherings, though, were tinged with aspects of bizarre superstition and mysticism. Many of the attendants followed the example of the ancients by swallowing pieces of flesh cut from the taisui in order to sample its effectiveness and share their experience with others. Even Lao succumbed to peer pressure, swallowing a small piece of the taisui under the encouragement of the rest of the group. According to the description in his diary, it was tasteless, like a weird gelatin or some sort of preserve. He personally held strong doubts as to the true effectiveness of the taisui, and so did not try it again. What really interested him was the taisui itself. Though the group's members frequently sliced off pieces from the taisui, the thing itself never changed much in size, just as the ancient books had described. Lao couldn't help but wonder if this phenomenon was the reason why people believed in the taisui's immortality-bestowing powers.

Yet the more he participated in these gatherings, the stranger their form and purpose seemed to become. At some point the discussion revolving around the taisui devolved into ridiculous idolatry, as people would unconsciously perform mad and obsessive worship before it. If Lao ever touched upon these actions, the others would immediately return to normal and dispel his concerns with amiable enthusiasm. This abnormal behavior filled him with concern. It seemed that everything he had seen before was just a charade in order to dispel doubt and appease newcomers: beneath their masks of normalcy was concealed a far more ominous intent. Lao could not help but think of that secret society of longevity that legend said had been created by the progenitor of the Lao family, which had passed through thousands of years and countless dynasties. Did they also, one hundred years earlier, worship a blob of peculiar water-dwelling flesh and plead with it to offer them an illusion of immortality? Where had the disciples of this sect gone following the disappearance of the Lao family? Had the sect continued to exist till the present, and if so were these mysterious gatherings its latest incarnation?

A much more tangible fear now began to grasp Lao and fill him with panic. During one of the gatherings, an attendee showed him a queerly shaped whistle and claimed that it had been used by the School of Longevity in its rituals during the late Qing dynasty to worship the taisui. They began to blow the whistle, and a wave of unprecedented horror washed over Lao — for he recognized that sound. It was the musical piping that he had heard intermingled with the faint sound of human voices all throughout those dark nights following his move into the old Lao residence. Lao's mind clouded with doubt as to the purpose of this group of people. Were they using the underground passageways beneath his house for clandestine activities? Perhaps their motivation for courting him was a hope that he could provide some assistance for these surreptitious undertakings? And what role had Luo Guangsheng to play in this? Considering the fanaticism of these people when confronted with the taisui, and everything he had learned about the School of Longevity and his ancestors, Lao sensed that he had finally seen the light, as the veil which had been cast over him was slowly pulled aside. Thus it was that during the Chinese New Year festival of 2013 he used the excuse of returning home to Jinan to cut off all contact with Luo and the other acolytes.

Although Lao Mingchang quickly broke off his relationship with the shadowy group, the old Lao residence in Qingdao continued to worry him. Once the New Year had passed, he began to dream of the house frequently. In his dreams the setting was not the present-day house that he knew, but the one in which his ancestors had lived long ago. He would even occasionally dream of a time before the house was built, when the ancestors of the Lao family still lived within the one small single-story building contained within the compound. Regardless of the veracity of his dreams, they exerted a powerful influence over him — constantly drawing his attention back to the old abode. So it was that in April 2013 he quietly moved back to the old house in Qingdao. The neighbors informed him that Luo Guangsheng and the others had not been spotted around the building, and this allowed him to relax to some extent.

However, this relief did not last long. Not long after moving back to the old residence, he once more heard whispering voices coming from underground during the dead of night. Yet the people active in the subterranean tunnels did not attempt to push open the trapdoor leading into the building — or perhaps they had already discovered it was now locked and did not wish to create any unnecessary disturbance. This still presented Lao with a difficult dilemma: on the one hand he wished to report these incidents to the police, but on the other he was worried about potential retaliation. After all, the clandestine activities had not really threatened him so far, and if his speculations were correct then those underground were already sure of his identity. True though this may be, the situation had undoubtedly left him a nervous wreck. On the pages of his diary he began to imagine what exactly was taking place in the underground tunnels, and wondered whether or not his ancestors had been involved in similar acts one hundred years earlier. Was it some kind of esoteric ritual? Or was there an underlying meaning even more mysterious and indescribable? He had once happened across a series of obscure and surreal passages within his great-grandfather's manuscripts that left the reader unable to judge what was true and what was exaggerated fancy. These thoughts plagued his sleep, twisting his nightly dreams into ever more execrable images where he plunged into unimaginable scenes and incredible places. Sometimes he glimpsed his ancestors and heard them deliberating trivial affairs that he had once read about in the old books, yet when he awoke the memory of the dreams would swiftly disappear, making it impossible to note down. There was one nocturnal image that left him feeling particularly upset. Though he could not clearly recall the dream once awake, he was certain that the ancestors he spoke with in his dreams were portrayed in the most monstrous and hideous forms — almost completely inhuman — though his dream-self knew them to be his deceased forefathers.

In July 2013 things began to take a more drastic turn, mutating in an irrevocably worse direction. The dreams about his ancestors increased yet again in frequency — even occasionally involving ancestors he had never previously encountered — so he ventured into the subterranean ancestral temple to check the sacred tablets. According to the records contained within the temple, the ancestors who appeared in his dreams had indeed existed, but he could not recall where he had seen their names. Then, on July 31, events escalated. That night he slept in the bedroom on the first floor. Sleep overcame him only after a great length of time, and when it did, atrocities crowded his dreams. As the clock approached midnight Lao awoke; but as he later wrote, he could not be certain whether he was truly awake or if what happened next was yet one more nightmare. Once again he heard the sound of human voices, as he had heard many midnights before: a cacophony of noise, though vague and indistinct. Hitherto the noise had always lurked at the edge of his hearing ... this time, however, he was certain that the sound was coming directly from downstairs.

He donned his jacket and quietly opened the door of the bedroom, leaving the lights off. Though the noise from below continued, nothing shone through the window save moonlight; everything was motionless. Most strange of all: he could distinguish nothing meaningful from among the voices — it sounded like the blabbering clamor of hundreds of people chattering in unison. The stench from the sewers swelled more than ever — enough to knock one unconscious. Lao had to force himself upright in order to reach the staircase. At that moment, somewhere in the murky half-light, he glimpsed something so terrifying that he almost fainted. Again he would later admit in his diary that what he saw was not truly real but a trick of the light from the moonbeams shining through the window, but at the time he thought that he had seen an enormous black shadow dashing past the foot of the staircase, a silhouette far larger than a human, an indistinct, featureless shade. The fragmented voices almost seemed to be emanating from the shadow — strengthening Lao's suspicion that the whole scene was nothing more than an illusion — though at the time he was frozen with fear, and could only stand breathless at the staircase, unable to even scream. The noises below continued for some time before gradually dissipating. After about ten minutes he recovered the use of his body and immediately returned to the bedroom, locking the door tight and remaining awake in bed till dawn.

Once day had fully arrived, he quietly crept downstairs and carefully checked all of the doors, windows, and the trapdoor leading to the underground tunnel; but they were all locked, with no sign of damage. There was no trace anyone had entered the house — the only evidence to hint at the occurrences of the previous evening was the suffocating stench that sent him reeling to open a window for fresh air. After completing his inspection, he wasted no time packing up his necessities and moving himself to a hotel near Qingdao Ocean University. He wrote in his diary that day that he was ready to leave Qingdao as soon as possible and wished to have no further involvement with anything concerning the old house or his ancestors. Obviously, this did not happen.

The entries in his diary over the following days were few and simple — mostly how he would return to the old residence during the day to check on the items he was planning to move out, and then at night retreat to the hotel for sleep. On occasion he would write about his dreams; but to the outside reader these are nothing but illogical ramblings. For example, on August 6 he claimed in his diary that he had dreamt of the entirety of his ancestors. In his dream they had stood together summoning him to cross over to them, then they had all merged together into one, transforming into a hideous multi-headed and multi-armed monster like the Hecatoncheires of Greek mythology. Following this, in his entry for August 9, Lao Mingchang abruptly wrote that the old house was exerting some kind of malignant influence over him. Every time he wished to leave Qingdao, he would quickly dismiss the idea due to some trivial matter. Not only that, he became ever more desirous to move back into the old residence. Even when he had no need to return to the house to check on his belongings, he found himself involuntarily drawn back to the building time and time again. Something terrifyingly instinctive within him kept reminding him that this business was not destined to conclude so simply. Whether it was magic or fate, he began to believe that at the old house some undiscovered secrets still lay in wait for him.

On the evening of August 11 he left his hotel like a ghost in the night and returned to the old residence with his luggage. He wrote:

It is two o'clock in the morning and I can hear

the sound of people moving downstairs. I do
not dare to open the door, but the sound does
not leave. I think they must have climbed up.
I can hear someone calling my name. Many
people. I have never heard these voices before,
but I know they are my ancestors. I can hear
the voice of Lao Gelin. I don't know how, but
I know it. I know that it is his voice. He is
calling me, calling me to go with him to the
Fairy Mountains across the sea.

This is the last legible entry in his diary. The entries
that follow are just paragraphs of trembling, scrawled,
and illegible words, smeared and unreadable. Several
neighbors, however, recall seeing Lao Mingchang on
August 12. On that day he seemed absent-minded, brain-
lessly repeating a few strange words like "I can't leave
the house" and "someone is waiting for me to return."
This was also the last time he was seen in person before
the residential committee worker found his body on
August 14. In addition, from the evening of the twelfth
to the thirteenth, several residents who lived close by
reported that they could hear an arrhythmic whistling
coming faintly from the old residence. The noise, however, did not last for long and did not surprise many
people, so nobody paid it any real attention at the
time. It was only after the discovery of the body that
people remembered the odd noise when questioned by
the police. According to one neighbor's recollection,
it was difficult to describe the sound in words — like
a shrill shrieking or an eccentric melody played on
a flute-like instrument or pipe, but at the same time

containing a series of barely pronounceable syllables. The otherworldly din could hardly be compared to any other known acoustic.

# 8.

Though it is my ardent hope that I may bring the reader a complete resolution to the tale of Lao Mingchang, I regret to say that neither the documents he left behind nor the inquiries I have made of his neighbors are enough to piece together a clear picture of what befell our hero. All they provide is a rough outline, with plenty of blanks for the imagination to fill in. As for the lingering unknowns, I can mention only a separate incident that took place a full six months after his death, through which lens we can steal a glimpse of this story's unhappy end.

As stated, all of the documents that were sent to the Shandong Provincial Cultural Relics and Archaeology Institute were processed and filed by the relevant staff. These documents were then, naturally, released within certain circles. Many people have read the papers left behind by Lao Mingchang, or have garnered a general understanding of the incidents that took place, but their views on the matter are varied and sundry. The mainstream view is that Lao attracted the hostility of a secret society, which led to his eventual death. At the same time, most people believe that the final bizarre passages of his diary were a sequence of hallucinations incurred by Lao's evident nervous breakdown — obviously with the secret society playing more than a starring role in the contrived supernatural impersonations that led to

his mental collapse. In February 2014, several researchers from the Shandong Provincial Cultural Relics and
Archaeology Institute returned to Lao Mingchang's
old home and ventured into the underground ancestral
temple in order to conduct a thorough investigation, and
simultaneously notified the Qingdao Municipal Public
Security Bureau about their findings. The authorities
displayed keen interest in the evidence at hand and
conducted multiple investigations on the secretive group
that the diary so frequently mentioned. By late March,
after determining the composition of the group, the
Public Security Bureau mobilized a police squad to
launch a rapid-search operation. Very little has been
released about the details of the operation, but what I
do know is that only a few peripheral members of the
group were arrested. The core of the group managed
to escape through the Qingdao sewer systems via a
passageway leading from their regular meeting place
before the police even arrived.

Owing to the crisscrossing pipelines of the old and
new sewer systems, the investigation became immensely
complicated and the number of officers assigned to
the case proved insufficient. Commanding officers
therefore made the decision to temporarily divide the
squad into ten units of two policemen each in order
to investigate the sewer system before backup arrived.
Each investigation unit was ordered to maintain radio
contact with central command. The dangers involved
with the situation were relayed to each unit, and they
were warned not to approach any fugitives without the
expectation of severe risk. Out of all ten units, however,
only the team that comprised officers Yin Zhou and Ma

Xiaowu[18] actually encountered anything of significance; all other teams came across absolutely nothing. And yet, the accounts given by these two officers were never included in any official report. Of these two witnesses, only Yin Zhou was willing to discuss the affair in detail with me — to this day Ma Xiaowu has refused to speak about what happened.

According to Yin Zhou's account, the two of them were assigned that day to explore one of the south-facing sewers. The pair walked for about ten minutes before gradually realizing that a peculiar scent had been growing more prominent among the filthy cocktail of sewer-system smells, though they paid little heed to it at the time. The umbra of claustrophobic pipes that enclosed them created the curious sensation that as they walked, they strayed further and further from the familiar world of light and deeper into a chthonic alien realm. Passing one of the larger pipes, Ma Xiaowu became aware of the almost imperceptible sound of human speech. The two officers signaled for backup before following the voices through an ancient and decommissioned pipeline. There was no water on the ground, though everything was slightly damp. And through the choking air of the revolting sewers, the singular odor they had sensed previously had been growing ever more overpowering, seemingly laced with omen. It was then that their torchlight fell upon a corpse collapsed at an intersection in the sewer pipes — one of the members of the secret

18    Yin Zhou and Ma Xiaowu bear more than a passing resemblance to Professor William Dyer and his colleague Danforth from *At the Mountains of Madness*.

society. The two officers had seen his photograph in a memo. He was sitting on the damp dirty ground against the wall of the passageway, head crooked, his face a strange bruised color — the complexion of someone long dead, beginning to putrefy. When Yin Zhou pulled out his radio to make a report, however, he leaned in for a closer look and saw that the body had developed some unspeakable changes.

Both officers gazed in astonishment, as the flesh and blood of the corpse transmogrified from solid matter into a viscous fluid. The skin that was exposed to the putrid air on the face, hands, and elsewhere now melted like a wax dummy under heat, exposing ashen bones beneath. The clothes enshrouding the corpse collapsed, and a dusky phlegm-like substance spread throughout the clothing of the deceased from the inside, oozing slowly from every orifice. At first the two thought it was blood, but no blood could reflect an iridescence that dark and greasy in torchlight. It was scarcely liquid at all, more like a flowing tar or slime. They then witnessed something even more unnatural. The torch illuminated the sticky mucus as it slowly gathered at the base of the corpse into one gelatinous pool, then — as though alive — extended and contracted, wiggling, and squirming its way deeper down one of the side passages. It has already become difficult for Yin Zhou to recall what his thoughts were at that time ... he felt enchanted, his mind a blank. He allowed the light from his torch to follow the crawling slime down into the depths of the sewer tunnels. As the light swept across the passageways it revealed even more bodies, bodies in a variety of different poses, all of them inexorably decohering, their corrupted bones protruding through. More pools of the black shining mucus marched along the sewer floor like macabre troops, wriggling in unison toward the deepest reaches of the sewer system. Then they saw something — the torch fully illuminated the passageway and the inescapable nightmare climaxed.

A seething mass of onyx oil! It swelled to unreckonable proportions in the malevolent shadow of the far distance, stuffing the drainage tunnel, unstoppable as the collapse of a mountain of black mud. The viscous agglutination flailed and bubbled in the torchlight, incessantly shifting between myriads of unfamiliar shapes and contours. The officers saw inordinate multitudes of grotesque glistening arms, claws, tentacles, and other unknown limbs stretching from and plunging into that hellish pile; innumerable grimacing wounds cracking open and sealing shut like mouths; and legions of viridian eyes forming like pustules, melting and popping across the ceaseless undulating of the creature's surface. Far more than a blasphemous imitation of nature! In the lapses between spewing protoplasmic organs, all of the arms, claws, and tentacles twisted and twirled through the fetid air, desperately grasping anything nearby. The mouth-like fissures screamed broken gibberish in an indistinguishable cacophony, while the temporary eyes rolled in the direction of the light source, glaring, unblinking, seeing. Amid the pandemonium, the infernal mass began to roll toward them like hot tar — swelling and trembling, eddying, pulsating! Screaming so loud that even its senseless din disappeared in the reverberations! It was the tight, staccato screech of a tortured pipe! It was the chaotic shriek of a sorghum whistle —

*"Tekeli-li! Tekeli-li! Tekeli-li!"*

The noise shook their basest survival instincts. At once the two men dropped their flashlights and bolted away in a frenzy. Already their memory is unable to recollect their thoughts or behavior from this time — as if that moment has been utterly erased from their minds. As the terrifying uproar echoed and dissipated amidst the passageways, other noises came now to their attention. Still more short blasts of wide-ranging piping, but these whistles came not from the horrendous atrocity clawing its way through the tunnel behind them. No, this piping echoed from the occulted depths of the labyrinthine sewer, locations even further distant, faint but still audible as the sound ricocheted up through the crumbling clay walls. The cries repeated, one after another, as if in response to those bone-chilling screams —

*"Tekeli-li! Tekeli-li!"*

The backup team found the two men in the darkness of a dried-out and abandoned drainage tunnel. Their nerves were shattered, and they were shaking so much they could barely string together a coherent sentence. The bodies discovered by the two officers were found by the rest of the police unit — every single one of them had decayed into a pool of black slime, identifiable only by their bones, in exactly the same state as Lao Mingchang's corpse had been found. Forensic investigation by the relevant authorities determined that the departed were indeed the intended targets of the raid; but to this day no definitive theory as to how the bodies could have decomposed at such an amazing rate has been forwarded. Likewise, there were no traces of evidence regarding the hideous monsters and animate black mucus as inadequately described by officers Yin Zhou and Ma Xiaowu. Most people believe they had inhaled too much of the toxic sewer air, so that when they had encountered the huge number of rotting bodies they hallucinated the affair from the pressure of their extreme mental stress. After three months of hospital treatment, Ma Xiaowu resigned and returned to his hometown. Yin Zhou remains in Qingdao, although he applied for a transfer away from the front line and now holds a menial position with no real responsibilities.

Neighbors of the old Lao residence hold various and unique views on the fate of Lao Mingchang and the old house, but these stories are too wild and fanciful to mention here. After Lao's death, many of the nearby residents relocated to other places; and now only two or three of the original households remain. Some may sneer at their irrational fear, but it may not be totally unreasonable. Just a few months ago, when I visited the police station on Jiangsu Road to review some of the investigation files, I overheard two young police-men discussing a very curious thing. They told me that during their previous evening's patrol of Dengzhou Road they had heard an odd noise emanating from one of the drains. Believing it to be somewhat similar to the noise of air passing through a narrow cylinder, they listened for some time ... but it wasn't exactly the same, for this sound recurred — and yet never repeated — in some kind of strange chaotic melody:

*"Tekeli-li! Tekeli-li!"*

*The End*

(Translator's note: "Taisui" — which literally means something like "Big Year" — has many meanings in Chinese that are difficult to convey in English. Its earliest meaning is connected with the planet Jupiter, which was the farthest planet known to early Chinese man. Jupiter was known as the "year star," and "taisui" originally meant the stars directly opposite Jupiter during its roughly twelve-year orbital cycle — whether Yuggoth was one of these stars is unknown. The Chinese system of the twelve-year cycle of animals was built from observations of these stars. When combined with the five elements of traditional Chinese thought, this twelve-year cycle is multiplied into the grand sixty-year cycle that governs all Chinese astrology. The individual years were later personified as sixty deities known as "taisui," or "year gods." "Taisui" is also the name given to a type of black fungus known as a lingzhi mushroom, of the *ganoderma* genus. The lingzhi mushroom is said to be influenced by the planet Jupiter and displays many of the remarkable regenerative properties of its counterpart in this story. It is frequently mentioned in old books such as *The Classic of Mountains and Seas* and was used in immortality elixirs during ancient times. There is also an ancient Chinese saying — "Do not dare to disturb the soil over a taisui's head" — which serves as a warning against those who seek to explore or provoke powerful unknown forces. Of course, in this story the taisui is something quite, quite different.)

Toward the end of the Historian's story I had dared to lift up the jar for closer inspection. The black wriggling thing encased within was indeed a small portion of this ... taisui, as the Historian had termed it. It was safe within its glass prison; furthermore, this was only a small piece taken from something much larger and infinitely more deadly, but I was wise to still exercise caution when in such close proximity to it. The Historian may have called this protoplasmic little slime a "taisui," but I knew it by another, older, name: a name that could instill terror into any who heard its dread sound. A curse upon those so-called Amphiura Gods who had brought this foul creation into the universe! Still, they had paid the ultimate price for their folly, and their kind roamed this world no longer. Their cities and their corpses lay dead beneath the devastating cold and ice of the mountains of madness.

I moved to place the jar back into the box. As I did so, I thought I heard the faint whisper of a strange and arrhythmic whistle ... though it was quite impossible. Choosing to move my thoughts on from the poisonous taisui, I pushed it into a dark corner of the box, and then carefully removed the final object from my collection.

Like the ashen grey scroll that the Researcher had brought back from the wilds of Sichuan, this was also *a scrolled parchment of unbelievable antiquity, though made from a different type of material and more closely resembling cloth. With great care, I unrolled it across the table that lay between myself and my four guests, revealing a curious and entrancing depiction of all manner of strange creatures seemingly engaged in worship around an octagonal frame.*

*"That is mine!" cried a voice from the opposite end of the room. Without even looking I knew it to be the voice of my final guest — the Anthropologist.*

*"You have taken that from me," he continued, "just as you have taken me and brought me to this accursed place! Release me!"*

*"And me!" cried the Researcher, who was soon followed by the Dreamer and the Historian.*

*"Zzzilence, all of you!" I shouted, my voice becoming shrill as I momentarily lost control of my temper. Realizing my lapse in concentration, I took a moment to calm myself and regain my former composure. Indeed, the room was warm and stuffy, far different from my customary environment, and the stifling heat of the room only served to agitate me.*

*"You are an anthropologist by training," I said calmly, pointing in the direction of the one who owned the parchment. "I too am an anthropologist of sorts, interested in the great movements of the past and how these movements have influenced us in the present. And as you have chosen Tibet as your field of study, so too have I chosen this country to explore its mysteries and better understand not only what has come before us, but what may also come after. From one anthropologist to another, will you not extend*

me the courtesy of helping me to further understand your marvelous discovery?"

"A discovery which you have taken!" shouted the Anthropologist.

I leaned over the old parchment, taking in its musty scent heavy with the accumulation of years and centuries. Did this academic truly know what he had discovered, or was he nothing more than a childlike fool, wandering amid the darkness until he had accidentally stumbled across something so terrible and insane that a true revelation of what it represented would shatter his feeble mind into millions of irreparable pieces?

"Share with me about this scroll and how you found it," I whispered. "Share with me and you have my word that you will leave this farmhouse tonight."

"And the rest of us?" asked the Dreamer.

"All of you," I replied.

The Anthropologist began to tell his story.

# The Ancient Tower

I OFTEN wonder how the ancient things in our midst might still affect us. A plaything from a hundred years ago could drive us into a bidding frenzy. A thousand-year-old pagoda could give one the impression of having aged ten millennia. A tomb from the Warring States period[1] strikes one dumb with amazement. And then there are those places tracing their origins to even more remote antiquity that instill in one a sense of unspeakable strangeness. A friend of mine, an archaeologist, once mentioned an ancient civilization — a collective of primitive men who had lived and died alongside many long-extinct animals. Modern humans could only search through fragmentary bones and artefacts to even know of their existence. I detected a subtle hint of fear beneath his words. Those early men had fallen by the wayside of the long river of life, no longer adjoining our path, leaving behind only an endless expanse of the unknown that raised doubts as to whether we could dare call them human.

And yet an ancient stone stupa has granted me a deeper and more alarming understanding of my

1    475–221 BC.

friend's intimated fear. Within its confines, I witnessed something that I have tried vainly to blame on a hallucination, brought about by some combination of altitude sickness and fatigue — because I lack the slightest evidence to prove that my experience was either true or credible. At times, I still recall in terror that ancient place, and the interminable history that we can only glimpse by sifting through forgotten relics, and I desperately realize the naïve folly of that fantasy.

The first time I encountered the ancient stupa was completely by chance. At the time I was on my way for my initial investigation of the customs and culture of Tibetans living in the Sanjiangyuan area.[2] Before then I had never really gone deep into the Qinghai–Tibet Plateau, my understanding of the region coming entirely from books by Gele, Nicholas Roerich, Gombojab

2    Sanjiangyuan (literally: "Source of Three Rivers") is an area of the Tibetan Plateau located in Qinghai Province. It is perhaps worth mentioning to those readers unfamiliar with Tibet that Tibet consists of much more than modern China's Tibetan Autonomous Region (TAR), which contains only about half of the Tibetan Plateau's landmass and around 40 percent of the total Tibetan population within China. Of the three traditional provinces of Tibet, only Ü-Tsang is in the TAR. The other two provinces of Kham and Amdo are spread across today's Qinghai, Sichuan, Gansu, and Yunnan provinces. This story takes place in the Kham region, on the border of southern Qinghai and the TAR.

Tsybikov, and others.[3] As the scenery around me became increasingly desolate I fell into a mixed mood of loss and unease — as if I was gradually moving away from normal everyday contact with the civilized world and in turn entering a realm of unchanging wildness and isolation.

On March 21 I hitched a lift with a truck driver and headed to a cluster of villages situated in the west of Upper Laxiu Township in order to prepare for the final stage of my expedition. The journey was most tedious. Outside the window the monotonous plateau scenery had completely lost any appeal it once held for me and I was feeling drowsy from the altitude sickness that had plagued me since stepping onto the plateau. That afternoon, as the sun was setting, a lake as calm and flat as a mirror appeared amidst the rolling hills to the northwest of the truck, rousing my interest at last. Though I could see only the section of the lake visible between the gaps of the low foothills, this was enough for me to conclude that it was indeed a very wide stretch of water. Through the valleys winding betwixt the hillsides that accompanied our road I beheld a mountain of immense height to the north of the lake. At that moment the setting sun in the west was cresting against the mountain's snowcap, bathing the white peak in an eerie shade of lavender. Down at the base of the mountain, a low rugged hill was

3    Nicholas Roerich and Gombojab Tsybikov were both early-twentieth-century Russian explorers of Tibet. Gele is a current-day Tibetan and deputy director-general of China's Institute of Social Economics' Tibetology Research Center.

sandwiched between the lake and the mountain itself, creating a steep transitory zone. Scattered throughout were enormous exposed grey rocks and sparse meadows of pale yellow that comprised the bulk of the plateau's landscape.

Then, in a stray moment, I noticed an unusual black silhouette within the hills somewhere on one of the steep cliffs that stood almost vertically on the lake's far shore. Cast against the backdrop of the distant mountains' lavender-hued snowy peaks, the outline of this dark shadow loomed unexpectedly. It appeared to be a low cylindrical tower capped with a dark, slightly rounded dome. Though it was difficult to see any more detail at this distance, the unusual outline indicated that I was undoubtedly looking at a man-made structure of some form — albeit one that stood without awkwardness in this uncivilized wasteland. On the contrary, something about the structure gave off a difficult-to-name sense of harmony with its surroundings of soaring cliffs, the placid lake framing the desolate land, and even the icy peaks to the north. It seemed destined to its part in the plateau, placed upon those steep cliffs as soon as this forsaken wilderness had been created. I was greatly disturbed by this abnormal sense of natural coordination, and quickly became afflicted by uncanny fantasies. Instinctively I believed that this was a building of immense antiquity — maybe even the great grandfather of the stone cairns that are dotted throughout the Tibetan landscape. Perhaps ancient survivors of the Great Flood had built it, or perhaps it harkened from an era older still when man barely stood over ape.

From the driver — his broken Chinese frequently

interspersed with outbursts of Tibetan — I learned that the mirror-like lake was known as Rongpo Tso.[4] It was an inland lake of considerable size and when the snows melted in spring and summer it could become even wider and stretch out to the unseen distance. When I asked the simple driver about the shadow on the cliff on the lake's far side he was struck with fear and anxiety. With a shake of his head he pretended to know nothing about the place before he stopped speaking altogether. Out of courtesy I ceased my questioning. The truck turned into a highway to the southwest so that the bleak hills nearby now blocked my view of the calm lake and the gloomy shadow lurking in the mountains. I was left alone to continue contemplating the scenery as before.

Later that day I arrived at Lung Mar, a small village next to the provincial road. It is a small settlement nestled in front of the mountains. If one passes through the village to the northwest, you will find yourself at the snowy mountains that mark the boundary between southern Qinghai and northern Tibet. The plains in front of the foothills are thinly scattered, with many low-rise huts made of stone and clay, though the area could never be called crowded. Although Lung Mar is said to be a village, in fact it is a settlement composed of several villages that have gathered together. There are more than one hundred households living there, most of which are engaged in rearing animals. Due to

4    Rongpo is a common Tibetan name. Tso means "lake" in Tibetan. Laxiu Township and Rongpo Tso are both real places in the western part of Yushu County, Qinghai Province.

its proximity to the road, most of its inhabitants sell cordyceps[5] and other highland specialties on the side. The truck driver introduced me to a family who lived by the road who often received passing visitors. More importantly, there was an old grandmother living there named Pasang Chungdak. Known affectionately by all as Granny Chungdak, she was the oldest living person in the area. This old lady was a treasure trove of folktales.

As I settled down that night, I couldn't wait to ask Granny Chungdak about local folklore. The old lady could understand only the simplest Chinese, so I had to interpret through her son Pemba Dorjee. Even so, I still managed to hear a lot of interesting local legends from them, but the stories they shared were disappointingly nothing new. I have heard many similar stories throughout my investigation into Tibetan folklore, all mainly variations on a combination of Tibetan Buddhism and local custom. The fables and legends impart lessons for daily life and those familiar with mythology should be able to detect the deeper meanings within these tales. Somewhere in my bored idleness I suddenly remembered the strange ancient tower that I had seen in the truck at dusk, so I politely asked them if they were aware of any legends surrounding it.

Upon hearing my request, Pemba Dorjee — a large Tibetan man with skin the color of bronze — was abruptly overcome with a look of peculiar terror. He

5    Cordyceps is a genus of parasitic fungi that attacks cat-
     erpillars, ants, and other insects. The resulting fungus is
     highly prized for its medicinal properties. It is commonly
     found across the Tibetan highlands.

did not translate my question to the old lady but with great anxiety asked me to talk of other matters instead. All he would tell me was that the local people refused to discuss the place because ghosts and evil spirits were trapped within, and that it would be better for me not to inquire any further about the edifice. Yet his warning failed to deter me and only further aroused my interest; I pressed him to tell me the story of the ancient stupa.

When he realized that he couldn't change my mind, Pemba Dorjee shook his head in despair. Turning to the old lady, he muttered a few words and rose, beckoning me outside the room. More than a little confused, I followed him into a cold narrow hallway, lit only by a dim oil lamp. Pemba Dorjee added some oil to it and placed it on a low wooden table, then sat face to face with me. He started by requesting that I ask Granny Chungdak no more about anything related to the old stupa, as the locals considered speaking of it extremely inauspicious. In exchange, he would personally tell me everything I wanted to know about the tower. However, he reminded me that the old stupa was exceedingly ill-omened, and that none should disturb it. I promised to heed his request and patiently recorded everything he said.

The legends surrounding the stupa related to me by Pemba Dorjee were numerous, but mostly fragmented, ambiguous and clearly influenced by aspects of Tibetan religion and superstition. Nevertheless, they still contained some singular and unexplained qualities that left me unable to completely turn a blind eye to them. To put it simply, the locals believed that evil spirits were imprisoned within the stupa — locked in the tower and unable to escape — but if someone was daring enough to enter there was no guarantee what might happen. To merely talk about the place was considered dangerous, since the spirits trapped within could invade people's dreams and exert a terrible influence upon them.

None of the legends elaborated on when the stupa was built, nor by whom, nor on the spirits imprisoned within. The only certainty was that the ancient tower had existed long prior to the village's foundation. Some of the legends said that before the establishment of the village a mysterious esoteric branch of Buddhism had conducted rituals in the area to worship the souls within the stupa. At the same time these legends also stated that the old stupa and the imprisoned souls were far older than the mysterious sect; and still more legends claimed that the spirits had existed long before the stupa itself. They had lurked in that place, grabbing any victims that should pass by, until a powerful sorcerer succeeded in trapping them and building the stupa to warn future generations. There were other bizarre old myths that said the stupa had actually been part of a gigantic city of an even older civilization, and that when it perished, its people hid within the stupa, where they were transmuted into spirits unable to leave. Regardless of the source, evidence for the souls trapped within the tower was not entirely groundless. The legend related by Pemba Dorjee included several stories about them, which were much clearer than the legends of the spirits and the old stupa's origin, and stood up to repeated telling.

The experience of a herdsman from several decades ago featured prominently in many of these stories. During the 1920s, a young man named Champa Phunt-sok ventured into the hills on the opposite side of the

Rongpo Tso while in search of a missing yak. As midnight approached he unwittingly climbed up the foothill where the stupa was situated. When the torch in his hand illuminated the gloomy tower close by, he immediately remembered the ominous legends that circulated among the elders of the region. The warnings fresh in his mind, he made haste to turn and leave the fearful place along the path that brought him there. As he did so he thought he heard the faint sound of something strange. The sound was indistinct, carried from afar by the wind, and unlike anything he had heard before, so he wondered if he was hearing something illusory. At first, he thought it was his own yak, so he yelled once or twice into the air but did not receive any form of response. Still the noise remained unchanged, so he plucked up his courage and threw a stone toward the tower. The stone smashed against the tower wall with a dull crash, and as soon as it did, a nerve-wracking scream issued forth from the bowels of the stupa, as though from somebody who had been frightened out of their life: toneless, wordless, and harrowing in the dead silence of midnight. Champa Phuntsok was scared out of his wits; rushing down the hillside, he ran wildly back to the camp where the herdsmen had gathered. Afterward he was overcome with a severe illness and almost died. His experience caused quite a stir in the local area, but the incident was gradually forgotten as time went by, re-emerging from the communal memory only when something similar reoccurred. It is said that on the second day of Champa Phuntsok's return to camp, several of the more courageous herdsmen climbed up the foothill during the light of noon to take a look at the ancient stupa. Nobody dared to approach that high place of foreboding once night had fallen, especially after seeing the distorted look of terror that was now etched upon Champa Phuntsok. However, their exploration proved fruitless. Neither the lost yak was found nor a single soul was seen — let alone anything that could have produced such a petrifying scream.

That night I could not sleep as I turned these strange legends over and over again in my mind and wondered how I could approach the local villagers about similar stories the next day. I remained in the guestroom until the day was bright, then I walked out of the house and plunged myself into a new day of fresh investigation. Through the course of the day I managed to collect local folktales, stories, and customs from the villagers, but I had already heard most of them from Granny Chungdak and Pemba Dorjee. Simultaneously, I gradually discovered that my interest was slowly shifting away from local customs and moving more and more toward the old stupa. Any hint of a story about the stupa was enough to rouse my interest, causing me to pursue ever-more-relevant questions.

Unfortunately, the fear that lurked within the community severely hindered my work in collecting these stories. On the one hand, the majority of these superstitious locals were reluctant to even mention that ominous place — so deeply had the tradition of avoiding the old stupa been imprinted upon their minds. Even those villagers brave enough to whisper any mention of the gloomy tower had little idea what sense of fear and evasion had first prompted their ancestors to form such a tradition. In all the tales that I managed to elicit, ghost stories accounted for the vast majority. In terms of time span, the earliest and latest stories were at least one century or one and a half centuries apart, but almost all of them contained some identical pattern or characteristic. As an example, all the stories concerning what happened to Champa Phuntsok spoke of the strange and obscure sounds that were heard near the stupa during the dead of night, and most of them also referenced that dreadful scream; some even spoke of more than one scream. I was left confused by this unusual set of circumstances, so that when I came to analyze the stories more closely I came to two separate conclusions. First, that the stories were derived from the same factual basis — in which case these odd sounds could genuinely be heard from an unknown source beside the stupa. Second, that the reports of spectral noises instead came from the same obscure ghost story — the original story pattern used to create modern derivatives to instill new fear in each successive generation. Though the protagonist may change from a pilgrim monk to a wartime deserter and finally to a wandering herdsman, the story essentially remained the same.

At the time I was quite proud of my own inferences, and I soon found an opportunity to prove my theory. That same afternoon I heard of a person who had been personally involved in a paranormal incident and was still alive. He was a Tibetan named Dawa Tsering and he lived in the small village of Chaba Gangca, situated about six miles from Lung Mar. It was said that he had once led a group of youths to investigate the stupa after a particular episode of ghostly activity. Although the investigation had failed to unearth anything, he could at least give me a chance to confirm whether some of the stories were true or not.

With this in mind, I hired a guide the next day to lead me to Chaba Gangca. The village was located on the side of the great lake, Rongpo Tso, which I had seen two days previously. It was much smaller than Lung Mar, with only a few dozen people living there. Perhaps due to its isolation and distance from the highway, the village gave me a deep feeling of ignorance, poverty, and timeless seclusion. The barley-growing land on the lakeside slopes seemed barren and forlorn, while the few houses scattered between the fields and mountain ridges all encapsulated the common features of remote villages everywhere — low, dark, and dilapidated. The village was even quieter than I had imagined. En route I saw old Tibetans, heavy with the suffering of life's vicissitudes, sitting alone in silence on the doorsteps of their tumbledown homes, their wrinkled dark-red faces obtuse and inscrutable, their eyes sleepy and lacking in life. All of this contributed to an indescribable sense of unease within me, halting my desire to step forward and make inquiries, as if I was moving closer to something ancient and forbidden.

The guide had to ask several families before he was able to find the address of old Dawa Tsering. It was a hut built from earth and rock on the slopes at the edge of the village. Even in this small, remote village, its dark and dwarven appearance seemed somewhat rundown. Upon our arrival, the old Tibetan man was sitting basking in the sun atop one of the slopes by his door. He did not express any surprise about my arrival, nor did he offer any form of welcome. In fact, he seemed totally indifferent to everything around him. Based on the stories I had heard and his mane of grey hair, not to mention his wrinkled face and toothless mouth, I guessed him to be around eighty or ninety years old. I greeted him respectfully as per Tibetan etiquette and explained the reason for my visit.

Perhaps it is due to my naturally respectful manner, but I found he seemed to enjoy my company. Even more of a surprise was that the old man could understand Mandarin quite well, though sadly he could speak only a few simple words himself, so we still required the guide to act as a translator. He told me that when he was young he once traveled to Xikang as part of a caravan.[6] He also worked as a soldier for many years and saw action on the battlefield, but later deserted after finding the bullying of his commanding officer insufferable. It was during these early years that he had learned some Mandarin, though his infrequent use of the language meant that he had forgotten most of it over the years. I mentioned that I had heard of the bizarre story involving him and asked him the truth of the matter. To my surprise, he did not seem to fear the gloomy stupa like the other locals. Instead, he admitted to me quite straightforwardly that he had indeed ventured into that place but had found nothing. As he related to me, this had all happened in those years following his desertion. At the time

6    Xikang was a province of the Republic of China comprising most of the Kham region of traditional Tibet. Most of it was incorporated into Sichuan Province after the founding of the People's Republic.

there was a wedding ceremony involving one of the wealthier local families, and two herdsmen decided to deliver some livestock as gifts. Due to the great distances involved, the herdsmen made up their mind to travel through the night in order to arrive with the gifts in the morning. Along the way they traveled round the lake, and upon passing the cliff where the ancient stupa stood, they heard the faint sound of unusual noises. The herdsmen were familiar with the legends associated around the stupa, so they knew immediately that the sounds were coming from the spirits trapped within. Shivering with fright, the pair began to recite loud chants of exorcism while spurring on the animals to hurry up and leave behind that disturbing locale. Later, on their route back home from the wedding, they circumvented the original path. Their ethereal tale caused a great commotion with the local herdsmen.

Fresh from his escape from the army, Dawa Tsering was young, reckless, and without fear. Hearing the story of the two herdsmen, the next day he gathered a group of daring youths to climb the hillside. Not only did they fail to encounter any spirits, they also did not hear any of the reported strange sounds. There was nothing to be found at all apart from the unimaginably old stupa itself and its gateway that had been long blocked by persons unknown. The blockade must have been constructed a very long time ago, because the rocks obstructing the entrance all showed signs of severe wind erosion. There was also a large hole at the top of the barricade, where some of the rocks had fallen over time. Since nobody else agreed to enter the stupa, Dawa Tsering climbed up the stone pile alone and entered the old tower through the hole. However, aside from one large *doubeng*[7] piled up within, the tower's interior was disappointingly ordinary with no strange sights to dazzle him. He turned around within the stupa; but since there was nothing remarkable to be found, he decided to climb back out the way he had entered. Just as he was about to begin his ascent, he chanced to discover a box pressed beneath one of the stones on the interior side of the blockade. The box was in an advanced state of decay after unknown years of lying in this manner; Dawa Tsering, however, could see it was wooden, roughly two feet in length, five or six inches thick, and that it looked like something that had once been used by a wealthy family to store precious objects. Using all his strength he pulled at the box to get it from under the rocks, yet because of its severe deterioration the wooden box collapsed completely, revealing a small package wrapped in oiled paper within. Opening the package, he discovered a *thangka*[8] painted on a piece of cloth. At the same time, the other youths who had accompanied him began to call his name from outside the tower, urging him to leave soon. Hurriedly

7  A *doubeng*, also known as a "mani heap," is a Tibetan cairn. They are normally manmade piles of stones placed in conspicuous locations for religious reasons.

8  A *thangka* is a Tibetan Buddhist painting on cotton or silk usually depicting Buddhist deities or elaborate religious imagery. Most thangka are intended for personal meditation or instruction of monastic students. If stored properly they can normally last for a very long time.

rewrapping the thangka, Dawa stuffed it into his clothes and climbed back up the blockade.

I could not help but feel a wave of excitement when I heard this, so I wasted no time in asking the old man if I could see the thangka. The old man hesitated for a while, then with a nod of his head agreed to my request. He turned and entered his low dwelling. Some moments passed before he appeared again at the door holding a scroll wrapped in animal skin. He told me that he had originally intended to sell the thangka to one of the explorers who had been prolific in Tibet during those years. Since he had just fled from the army and had not brought any of his belongings back with him, the thangka would have been an ideal way to raise some money. Yet after showing it to several explorers, they all concluded that the thangka was nothing more than an eccentric fake. Nobody was willing to purchase it, at least not for anything more than an abysmally low price. As he was unable to ever come to an agreement with any potential buyers, he never succeeded in selling it. After a while, Dawa Tsering's life gradually stabilized, so the thought of selling the thangka never reoccurred to him.

When I unfolded the thangka from the animal skin, I realized that it was indeed a most peculiar thing. The more I looked at it, the more surprised and confused I became. My surprise and confusion came neither from the texture of the thangka nor the painting technique used in its composition. Based on these two aspects alone, the thangka was an example of excellent craftsmanship, albeit one that was no longer in good condition. Some of the colors woven into the thangka had fallen off, and the entire canvas was covered in signs of damage or impending decay. As for its painter, although the thangka had no indication that it had been produced by the hand of anybody famous, it nevertheless displayed a level of accomplishment considerably higher than most of the other folk paintings I had seen. Yet the content of the thangka itself was bizarre beyond my imagination and left me stunned for the longest time.

Since the picture did not feature any of the of the typical patterns and symbols of Bon[9] or Tibetan Buddhism, I assumed that this was no ordinary religious thangka. Its content violated the most basic laws of logic and common sense, making it difficult for to me to classify it as a narrative thangka. In total it was two and half feet long and less than two feet wide. Painted on both ends of the thangka was the decorative pattern typically seen in the western part of Tibet's Kham region. In the center of the thangka was a gold octagonal frame, its borders bursting with a multitude of people and indescribable inhuman creatures. About half of all the people visible were Tibetans. Strangely, the clothes and attire of these Tibetans did not belong to the same period, but were in fact spread out over a vast expanse of time. Some of the costumes reflected the characteristics of the Tubo Kingdom[10] or earlier. Others were more akin to modern Tibetan dress, with some of the features of attire that Tibetans would have worn during the Ming and Qing

9    Bon is the traditional animist religion of Tibet. It predates Buddhism and is still practiced in some areas.

10   The Tubo Kingdom was the great Tibetan empire that flourished from the seventh century to the ninth century, when the Tibetan plateau was unified.

dynasties.[11] Stranger still were the portraits of those people who were not Tibetan. These people did not wear the same type of clothing, nor did they even belong to the same race. Within the sea of faces I noticed Han Chinese, Mongolians, and still others, who were typically Caucasian with Aryan faces. Still others had more uncertain ethnic features, making it difficult to determine their true origin. The most disturbing and puzzling images in the entire thangka were the non-human things. There were at least four or five entirely different species. Depicted in the lower-left corner of the octagonal frame were some grotesquely anthropomorphic serpentine creatures. They resembled snakes but stood erect and upright, their slender bodies and necks supplemented by legs and arms covered in scales and wearing the most outlandish clothing. In the lower-right corner of the frame were black-snouted winged creatures of strange birth, resembling gargoyles from a Gothic church. Further up, in the upper center of the thangka, there was a peculiar design that looked like something approaching a giant cone-shaped sea anemone with four thick tentacles protruding from its tapered top. There were many other strange designs like this, but I have never seen anything like them on other Tibetan paintings nor have I heard of similar things within Tibetan mythology. Some of those images reminded me of ancient legends I had read in my younger years. Those obscure myths of dubious origin had without exception been of a sinister and evil nature, but they had all told of an ancient world existing long before the emergence of man. Outside the

11   Ming dynasty: 1368–1644. Qing dynasty: 1644–1912.

octagonal frame the remaining narrow space was filled with paintings of exotic buildings and scenery. Most of them were very abstract, making it difficult for me to identify their specific meaning. Yet something in the way these images were arranged made me think of the Buddhist maps of reincarnation that are so often seen in Tibetan temples.

All of the people and anthropomorphic monsters shown on the thangka seemed to be worshipping something. Crowded within the octagonal frame, they stood together, forming a huge circle. They faced the center of the octagon, some prostrating themselves, some clasping their hands together, others reaching out their arms or bowing at the waist ... but all focused on the act of worship. However, in the center of the octagon — in that place they were all facing — there was nothing. I could almost see the remains of some paint there in the blank center of the thangka; but for whatever reason the painting that had once existed there had been erased, leaving only a blank.

This bizarre content caused me to fall into a deep state of bewilderment. This thangka appeared to be connected with that secret religion spoken of in legend; its scenes of esoteric worship interspersed with non-human monsters originating from the same occult teachings. Many religious paintings depict the birth of certain important characters as linked to animal worship; a connection that implies all creatures and life enter the world from the same point of origin. The idolatry performed by the monstrosities implied that whatever man or being they were worshipping was seen as very special and imbued with great importance. Still, the mystery of the differently attired Tibetans and those worshippers of other ethnicities only plunged me further into confusion.

With Dawa Tsering's permission, I took some photographs of the inexplicable thangka. Afterward I asked him for other examples of myth and folklore circulating in the local area, but to no further gain. Then, in order to gather more folk materials and local legends, I extended my expedition by several days. Finally, on March 30, I hitched a ride on a passing truck back to Yushu and from there continued to Xining[12] by car. I boarded a plane and left the Tibetan Plateau, thus ending my expedition.

After returning to the university where I worked, I gathered several friends who specialized in regional history and mentioned the unexpected stories I had unearthed. I asked them for their assistance in helping me find some academic materials related to the legendary sect. This request, however, did not progress as smoothly as I hoped. There was scant information regarding this esoteric religion and even less that could determine its age. It was not until almost two months had passed before I received the information I desired. Up till then I had sought out multiple scholars, collectors, and art historians specializing in Tibet, asking each and every one of them to ignore the content of the painting and focus on deducing the age of the thangka by meticulous analysis alone. This proved to be a difficult challenge, as due to the extraordinary weirdness of the images most experts insisted that it was a modern work as soon as

12 Xining is the capital of Qinghai Province and the largest city on the Tibetan Plateau. The county of Yushu lies around five hundred miles away.

they set eyes upon it. Only a single old academic who had lived in Tibet many years before was able to detect some clues from the pigmentation and brushstrokes used on the canvas; but even then he still told me with a firm sense of conviction that the thangka was just a quirky and novel piece of recent creation.

On May 21, a friend of mine who studied the regional history of the Kham region provided me with a set of documents that focused my attention once again on the ancient stupa and the shadowy legends associated with it. The documents were taken from the biography of a native chieftain — or "*tusi*" — from the Kham region. Although the biography was relatively short, its authenticity seemed reliable. It led me to think back to those arcane, mystery-shrouded teachings and the ethereal legends connected with them. The Tibetan documents were difficult to understand, so I will only generalize their contents here.

These documents were related to a Tibetan named Tsesong Gyalpo, who was a native chieftain during the reign of the Qing Emperor Kangxi.[13] The fiefdom he inherited approximately encompassed modern-day Upper Laxiu Township in Qinghai Province and the northern part of Quna District in Tibet proper. According to the documents, this person was extremely superstitious and easily influenced by stories of ghosts or paranormal activity, as well as being a supporter of many Buddhist lamas and Bon shamans. One day he went out for a stroll and when passing by a certain place he happened to hear a powerful shaman preaching, so he made a detour

13   1661–1722.

to listen to the shaman's words. Yet after hearing the shaman's sermon, he realized that the words and deeds of this particular soothsayer were entirely different than anything else he had heard from other monks and shamans before. Not only did the shaman's words ooze with truth, but he also knew many things totally unknown to others and could recite the wildest and most amazing stories. After the shaman had completed his sermon, Tsesong Gyalpo wasted no time in inviting him to his residence with the hope that he would be regaled with even more curious tales. So it was that the lamas and the Bon acolytes who had previously enjoyed the patronage of the chieftain came forward to challenge the shaman. Needless to say, the newly arrived shaman was unruffled by these impotent rivals and saw off their challenges with ease, greatly pleasing the chieftain, who rewarded the shaman handsomely.

For several days, the shaman stayed at the residence of Tsesong Gyalpo and recounted at length many a strange tale that the chieftain had never heard before. Fascinated by the bewildering and bizarre stories, the chieftain asked the shaman where he had heard such fantastic tales; but each time the shaman avoided answering. That was until one day, when the shaman accidentally blurted out the name of a place called "Sipasa" halfway through the recital of one story. After uttering the name, the shaman admitted that all of his singular knowledge came from this region. Upon hearing this, the chieftain immediately asked the shaman to take him there for a look. At first, the shaman did not reply to Tsesong Gyalpo's request, but eventually after repeated appeals and demands, he consented to take the chieftain there.

The two men rode their horses west for a whole day until they arrived at a large lake. The shaman asked the chieftain to rest in the lakeside village until nightfall when he would bring the chieftain to "Sipasa." The local villagers received the chieftain with a warm welcome, telling him that all of the people living in the area were of the same sect as the shaman. This land was the sacred land of their sect, and the gods who they worshipped had left them this strange sanctuary known as "Sipasa." If a person entered that temple at the right time, they would be able to see the flow of all life and death: the life cycle of the entire world.

This only served to intrigue Tsesong Gyalpo even more. Still he urged the shaman to take him to that wondrous place, but the shaman firmly insisted that they proceed only after nightfall. They waited until the sun had set and the land was completely covered in darkness. The shaman held a torch aloft in his hand and led Tsesong Gyalpo to the hill by the lake, where stood a stone tower of great antiquity. The shaman waited for a while in front of the stupa, and after triple-checking the position of the stars overhead lit a single stick of incense. He informed Tsesong Gyalpo that no matter what happened, he could stay within Sipasa only for the time it took the incense stick to burn out, and that he must leave immediately before the incense expired. If he failed to do so, not only would his life be in danger, but he would be trapped within the stupa forever, doomed to repeat the same identical actions again and again for eternity. After the shaman had received Tsesong Gyalpo's solemn oath that he would abide by the rules, he finally led the chieftain into the stupa. As for what was within the stupa, the documents do not say. However, in his biography the chieftain inscribed a single short paragraph that describes his feelings after visiting the sacred sanctuary. The text is elusive in its meaning, so I have decided to just translate it in its entirety. The full text is as follows:

> That night at Sipasa, I saw with my own eyes the wheel of life turning. Countless kingdoms and dynasties rising and falling, forever in flux, yet always transient. I know now that mankind is but fleeting and of no consequence.

Tsesong Gyalpo was deeply affected by the journey, and without any hesitation he re-approached the shaman, offering him an obscene amount of treasure to bring him once more to that place. The shaman was unable to persuade the chieftain against the idea, so after selecting the most opportune time brought him once again to that hillside in the dead of night. In the shadow of the stupa he lit the incense and warned the chieftain to return before the stick was finished. The chieftain agreed and so the two entered the stone tower together. After this journey, the chieftain returned home and added these lines to his biography:

> I saw that monstrous host of gods and devils with their twisted forms and abnormal shapes, and other such things as cannot be described. When the incense approached its end, I fled, as if waking from a nightmare.

Only a few days had passed when Tsesong Gyalpo's desire to enter Sipasa erupted once more. This time, however, no matter how much the chieftain tried to bribe or coerce, the shaman was unwilling to take him there anymore. Moreover, the shaman warned the chieftain that he would die if he ever entered that place a third time. The furious chieftain had no choice but to return home. Before long, however, the chieftain summoned the shaman to his residence, and while the shaman was away from his village used the opportunity to secretly return to the stone tower. Since he was a *tusi* nobody dared to stop him, and he was able to enter the stupa alone. He was never seen alive again. When the shaman hurried back to the village, he found that the chieftain had already suffered a terrible death within the walls of the stupa. Following this incident, the position of *tusi* was passed down to the son of the chieftain, who immediately banned the sect, ousted its devotees from the lakeside village, and recovered all of the gold and silver treasures that the previous *tusi* had bestowed upon them. Any remaining objects pertaining to the cult were thrown into the stupa. The stupa was then ordered to be sealed and all were forbidden from ever entering it again.

Thus read the documents. Once I had understood the meaning contained within, I became instantly fascinated with the esoteric sect that was mentioned. It was clear that the incidents cited in the biography were consistent with the story told by Dawa Tsering: each confirmed the other. Dawa Tsering had seen the evidence that the stupa had been permanently blocked since that time, and the thangka found in the box must have been thrown into the tower succeeding the incidents recounted in the biography. The documents had mentioned that the sect referred to the stone tower as "Sipasa," causing me to reflect that this was a most unusual name. In Tibetan, "sipa" means "reincarnation" and "sa" means "place," the full name meaning "the place of reincarnation." The reason the stupa had been bestowed with this name was already lost amidst the passing of time, but it was obvious that Tsesong Gyalpo had seen something inside it, and that "something" had stirred his curiosity to the extreme.

Over the next few days I anxiously reviewed any literary or historical materials relating to the biography. My whole body was seized with a desire to uncover the secrets hidden in that mysterious ancient stupa. Yet despite my efforts over that time, my work failed to show any substantial progress. Though I did succeed in locating some fragments of information relating to the sect from local archives, nothing within them was particularly noteworthy. Eventually I realized that I would not gather any more information working in this fashion, so I began to plan a detailed and thorough field trip that would finally reveal to me the concealed mysteries of that enigmatic old tower.

On June 2 I flew to Xining Caojiabao Airport, traveled by car to Yushu County, then headed to Upper Laxiu Township. By the morning of June 7 I had arrived at Lung Mar Village, where I stocked up on final provisions. I then hired a guide to take me back to Chaba Gangca. That evening I stayed in the house of one of the local villagers and asked him about the nearby road conditions. When morning came, I carefully observed the landscape on the opposite side of Rongpo Tso with a telescope, systematically studying the structure of the mysterious stupa for the first time. My observation revealed something highly unusual: the stupa was actually a mixture of two different architectural styles. Both the dome and the upper part of the stupa were simple structures made from rough earth and stone, but the lower two thirds of the tower were composed of the thick walls common to Tibetan architecture. This seemed to indicate that the old building had been abandoned on more than one occasion. Perhaps it had first been constructed by a very ancient group of Tibetans, but for whatever unknown reason they had given up on its completion. Then that sect so often spoken of in legend and local historical and literary documents had appeared, converting it into a holy place for themselves. However, due to the limitations of my telescope I was unable to determine further exactly when the thick tower had been built.

Following my observations, I began to ask the villagers if anyone was willing to serve as a guide and lead me to the stupa. Yet as soon as word of my request got around the villagers, they began to chatter among themselves about the ominous stories of legend and insisted on entreating me to give up on this dangerous idea. When they realized that they could not dissuade me, all they could do was shake their heads and gaze at me in fear and unease as if they were confronted with one doomed to suffer the most horrible misfortune. This was not unexpected; the locals were only obeying the fear they had inherited from their ancestors. Even speaking about the ill-omened tower was an act deliberately avoided by them, though they knew not why. Thus, for them, the best course of action was to leave the stupa alone and ignore it entirely. Still, I was not worried about losing my way in pursuit of the stupa. I only had to follow the shore of the lake around and I would eventually arrive at the hill where the ancient tower stood.

Bearing this in mind, I set out to depart Chaba Gangca at 8 a.m. on June 9 just as the sun was rising. The plateau was still freezing cold at this time of the morning, so I put on the warm clothing that I had carried with me and packed a blanket into my backpack that I had bought from the villagers. I also brought along enough dry provisions to last me several days: flashlights, ropes, a pair of binoculars, tape measures, and assorted other items that I might need in event of emergency. I even packed a Tibetan knife just in case I met with any ... *special situations*. Based on my earlier observations, I estimated I was about six to eight miles from my goal. Under normal circumstances I would need only three hours to complete the journey, but here on the high plateau the lack of oxygen made the trek much more difficult. I would have to slow down and stay strong accordingly.

The scenery that accompanied my journey was monotonous and tedious. In the distance, the snow-covered peaks rose like waves beneath the great blue sky and constantly loomed ahead without the slightest change, the smaller foothills undulating closer by. Sporadic large meadows, awash in yellow and green, decorated the barren rocky hillsides that were otherwise devoid of life. Surrounded by this almost terrifying silence, the only thing I was able to distinguish was the rustling sound of the lakeside gravel beneath my footsteps. I kept the broad and placid expanse of Rongpo Tso always on my right side; it resembled a huge mirror reflecting the empty blue sky, with rarely a ripple to disturb its calm. The water in the lake was as cold as ice and gave off an unpleasant chill. Looking down into the water I could see neither fish nor waterweed. Though I was skeptical about what kind of creature could survive in such a cold lake, I was nevertheless uneasy about a lake so vast that it could not be comprehended in just one gaze. That's not to say I was afraid of some hideous monster lurking in the lake's depths; rather it was instinctual fear of the unknown. I was more at ease when I saw the occasional trace of herdsmen having passed through the region — at least it proved that I wasn't alone in having visited this land.

At 11:30 I stopped to rest for a while, replacing my thick winter jacket for something more suited to the rising temperature. I had already completed half of my journey by this time and was already on the opposite side of the lake, yet still far behind schedule, and so quickened my pace. Behind me the houses of Chaba Gangca village were almost imperceptible; only some barely distinguishable fields spread out across the hillsides hinted at the settlement's existence. It was then that I suddenly realized that quite some time had passed since I had last seen any trace of humanity. This caused me to once more experience that sensation of loss and discomfort I had felt when first entering this highland wilderness — a sensation that made me feel I was in an empty world, facing an endless and unknown wasteland alone. I needed to leave these disturbing and unsettling thoughts behind me, so I ate some of my dry provisions then set off again immediately.

At approximately two in the afternoon, I finally arrived at the base of the foothill where the mysterious stupa stood. The foothill was only about fifty feet high, but the slope facing me was extremely steep with many small shrubs and weeds growing upon it. There were few places that offered a foothold upward, so I was forced to circumnavigate the base of the hill and hope that I could find a more accessible side to climb. I soon found that the slopes on the northwest side of the foothill were smoother in comparison to other directions, and with frequent clumps of weeds that could provide a handhold. An age must have passed since the last living human or animal had ventured up to the gloomy stupa, as there was no trace of either as having climbed this slope. Due to my heavy load I had no choice but to take the gentlest and easiest slope for my ascent. When I finally made it to the top of the hill, I found it to be an almost-flat, almost-circular plateau of about one hundred feet. Mud of yellow and brown covered the barren ground, with a scattering of short wilting weeds poking through the dirt. Compared to some of the nearby granite peaks, this hill was clearly covered in a large amount of topsoil that hid the granite underneath. Surveying the surrounding landscape, I could see that to the west of the hill were some low stone walls, lying either broken or in ruins — the only trace of prior human habitation. On the opposite side of the hill were the broad and calm waters of Rongpo Tso. From this side of the water I was able to glimpse some low-rise dilapidated buildings and fields with signs of cultivation scattered across the hillsides; that must have been Chaba Gangca village.

Most curious of all was the imposing ancient stupa itself, situated on the southeastern corner of the hill and seemingly about twenty-five to thirty feet high. The overall shape was like a cylinder — or more precisely, an octagonal cylinder — with the upper sides of the wall progressively contracting at the top. Fascinatingly, the structure was a mixture of three distinct architectural styles, not the two I had previously assumed. The stupa's highest point — the same I had distantly espied before through my telescope — was a simple structure of earth and stone, somewhat darkened by the passage of time. Two-thirds of the way up, the simple earth-and-stone construction was gradually replaced by a thicker, sturdier wall of greater refinement. There was a clear demarcation between the styles but not always at the same level; in some areas the thick wall was higher, and in others it was lower. This seemed to confirm my previous assumption that the stupa had been first abandoned then rediscovered by a later group who added their own repairs and improvements onto the original. The style of this part of the stupa was very close to that of common Tibetan architecture with its thick walls and how it narrowed toward the top. The walls were dry and had been made by stacking together large stones, then filling the cracks with gravel; the exterior was paved over with pasty red clay. Despite its great age the tower was nevertheless immensely strong. The paint on the walls had long since peeled off, revealing the original dark color underneath, but in some of the wall's depressions it was still possible to see some scraps of white paint.

What really interested me was the base of the tower. The architectural style of the tower changed significantly once again about three feet from the ground. Whereas the original style featured large stones cemented together by gravel and red clay, the base of the tower was clearly much more like a regular octagon in its outline. It is worth noting that the stones at the base were very thick; about one-third thicker than the already sturdy Tibetan style walls above. These boulders had eroded to a much greater extent than the hybrid walls built above them, making it hard to imagine what they had originally looked like. Even so, those features that had survived time's relentless onslaught proved that those who were behind this construction had possessed surprisingly superior skills in the masonic craft.

There were no windows on the stupa; the only portal to the outside world was the gigantic entrance on its northwestern side. The gate, which was easily ten feet high and six feet wide, was blocked by a large pile of stones, leaving only a small hole about three feet from the ground as a potential entry point. It must have been built in the same period as the base of the tower, because they both had the same architectural features: regular, huge, and flat. Two immense obelisks formed the frame of the gate, while a separate rectangular granite block about six feet long sat upon the two obelisks to form the threshold.

It would be difficult for me to climb the rocky pile with the large amount of things that I carried with me, so I decided to expand the hole a little first in order to make it easier for me to enter. This was a simple task: all I had to do was push the topmost stone and let it roll to the bottom. My actions were somewhat disrespectful and ill-omened; but since no one else had dared to climb this gloomy foothill with me, I was willing to compromise my scruples. Simple as this task was, altitude sickness slowed me down considerably. For two hours I busied myself expanding the hole until it was big enough for me to walk through upright. Once I had done so I was able to survey the interior of the stupa for the first time.

Due to the thickness of the walls, the space inside the tower was not as large as it appeared on the outside. As old Dawa Tsering had said, apart from a stone pile in the center of the room and some black rotten wood, there was nothing at all that caught the eye on first glance. I realized that the floor within the stupa had been laid out at the same time as the external base had been constructed, since the enormous stones used were identical. The originally flat ground had become pockmarked with the passing of the years and was covered with gravel and clay that had fallen from above. The roof of the stupa had long since collapsed; giving the illusion when viewed from a distance that one was looking at an oblate dome. Light came in from a hole about a dozen feet below the ceiling; I hadn't noticed the hole before but the light that poured through it illuminated everything within the stupa. Considering that the simple earth and rock construction forming the upper part of the tower was too weak to support a vault, I guessed that the stupa's interior had originally contained a wooden structure as support in order to disperse the weight of the tower's peak. Quite possibly the wooden structure had decayed and collapsed over time, bringing the ceiling down with it. The large pieces of dead wood on the floor seemed to support my speculation.

My careful inspection of the stupa's interior completed, I felt more than a little disappointed. Exposure to the open air caused by the collapse of the ceiling made the environment most unsuitable for the long-term preservation of objects. Anything perishable like paper, cloth, or small wooden objects would have decayed into dust; even those tiny artefacts that had survived were corroded beyond recognition, leaving only a few imperishable remnants. After some thorough searching and rummaging I was able to find several small ornaments made from Tibetan silver, some broken wood left over from decayed everyday utensils, a few scraps of rotten thangka, and a handful of other odd little objects. Nothing that I found offered any clear correlation with the secretive cult, nor was there anything close to an idol or symbol of worship. However, the carving of most of the metal ornaments I found was similar to those of other Tibetan handicrafts dating from the reign of Emperor Kangxi, so I was certain that the stupa had indeed been blocked up during that time as stated in the chieftain's biography.

By the time I had finished searching the stupa it was almost dusk; hence I decided to spend the night in the ancient tower and make further plans in the morning. After making up my mind, I climbed down the hill to look for some kindling and straw that could be used to make a bonfire. While I was down there I took another look at the ruins by the foot of the hill that I had seen previously, but I found nothing of interest. As was the case with the stupa's interior, there was almost nothing left amidst the ruins, just a few stone walls and rotten wood to prove that human life had ever existed here. After collecting some firewood I returned to the stupa, swept out a space beside the wall nearest the blocked entrance, lit a small bonfire for warmth, and finally settled down to eat some of my provisions. I grabbed the thickest winter jacket from my backpack to protect myself from the cold night. After all this work, I gathered up all the blankets I had brought, lay out my backpack, and slowly drifted to sleep against the corner of the blockade.

I do not know how long I slept, but when I awoke again the fire had already extinguished. The only light in the tower was the white light of the moon leaking in from the hole in the ceiling. This faint moonlight was enough to illuminate the entire stupa, though my surroundings were still as dark as before and I could only just make out the vague outline of my belongings beside me. The temperature was low and had left me freezing cold; no wonder I had awoken at the time I did. It was at this moment that I seemed to hear the faint sound of something in the ether. At first I thought it must be the wind coming in over the mountains, as there was always a lot of wind blowing through these mountainous regions during the night and it could create a variety of unimaginably strange sounds as it passed through. Yet the sounds were short and unclear, repetitive but with subtle changes, like the cry of something or some *things* conscious ... and I realized with a start that it could not be the wind. Immediately I sprang up and quietly reached inside my bag to find my flashlight and knife; preparing myself to deal with any unexpected situation.

It was then when the stupa suddenly screamed — a short, loud, and wordless scream violently rising to a crescendo then ceasing as abruptly as it had begun. Though the shriek was wordless and meaningless, I understood without any doubt that it was for certain the scream of somebody extremely frightened. Something peculiarly and indescribably familiar about that scream chilled me to my bones. Instinct took over long before my rational side could even fathom any appropriate response. Plunged into nameless fear, I grabbed the flashlight, scrambled over the pile of rocks, and ran as fast as I could out of that tower and as far as possible from its dark entrance. It was only when I reached the edge of the plateau that I realized there was nothing behind me and so came to a stop. The scream had long ceased, but other more haunting sounds continued their turmoil. For ten minutes I stood on the edge of that cold and piercing hilltop under the frigid night air, waving my flashlight toward the stupa's shadowy gateway while shivering uncontrollably with cold or fear — I am not sure which. At length I realized that these were the grotesque sounds of the spirits trapped within the stupa as told by so many ghost stories.

Cautiously, I covered every inch of the hilltop with my flashlight, but I found no human, no animal, not even anything that could move. The noises were as tempestuous as before; though they appeared muffled by something and much weaker than those I had heard within the stupa. Plucking up my courage, I conducted a more detailed inspection around the ancient tower with the flashlight, though I was still unable to determine the source of the noise. And yet, the more I listened, the more certain I became that the noise originated from the stupa's interior. It was muffled, exactly as it should be if passing through a very thick object before reaching my ear. I retraced my steps to the front of the tower and debated with myself whether I should go in and take a look.

Illuminated by my torchlight, the entrance to the ancient stupa was like a gateway to another world. Only an impenetrable darkness lay on the other side of the entrance apart from the multitude of indistinguishable cries that flew out of the tower and penetrated my ears. It was impossible not to believe that a host of evil and malignant things were lurking in the darkness out of sight. After much consideration and reconsideration, I hastily scrambled up the stone blockade leading to the entrance, deliberately making as much noise as possible. I did this not only to rouse my own courage, but to also alert — or should I say, intimidate — those screaming creatures that hid beyond the reach of my torchlight. The moaning, however, did not stop; but neither did it increase or become any more frightening. Rather, it remained exactly as before: like the clamor of a crowd or the chanting of believers at a Tibetan religious assembly. When I reached the top of the rocky pile I did not rush down into the stupa; instead I remained there and shone my flashlight carefully into every corner of the derelict interior.

Yet there was nothing within the stupa that could have made those incoherent sounds. Clearer certainly, but only because I was closer to the source of the noise rather than at the origin itself. Everything within the tower lay exactly as it had been during the day without the slightest change. Apart from the wailing unintelligible groans, there was no sign at all that the evil spirits mentioned in the local ghost stories were still active. Gathering my strength, I willed myself to pick up a stone from the pile and throw it against the inner wall opposite me. In an instant I heard the clear sound of the stone hitting the far wall, but for the reaction it provoked I might well have thrown a fistful of mud. The disjointed and jumbled noises neither ceased nor increased, but just continued in their endless cacophony like the sound of wind blasting through the mountains or the tide of the sea — entirely indifferent to the outside world. After realizing this fact my fear gradually decreased: confusion and curiosity now overpowered my survival instincts. Relieved, I crept down the blockade into the stupa and picked up my backpack. Then I sat down in a manner that made it easy for me to stand up and flee at any moment.

I was deluded if I thought I'd be able to sleep again. Nestled between my winter jacket and blanket, I tried to distinguish the different sounds within that intermittent and ever-changing commotion. The sounds were unclear at first, and difficult to tell apart; but when I held my breath and began to listen carefully the original dissonant tumult became more identifiable. I could make out the voices of Tibetans reciting scriptures together as well as some peculiar squealing. Most of the noises, however, were just too bizarre for me to even imagine where they could have come from. During this period I also heard more than a few exclamations and shouts. Though I was shocked and frightened by these sudden loud sounds, I was much calmer than when I had heard that first scream.

I tried to blame my earlier fears on being unprepared for the abrupt and unexpected scream, knowing in my heart that this was not the case. The initial scream seemed to have contained some unnamable trait that I couldn't quite put my finger upon — I had felt the mad fear of whomever had emitted that scream. Curled up by one corner of the blockade, I squatted worriedly for half the night until about four or five o'clock. The sounds gradually became fainter, till at some point I suddenly realized that the noise had ceased and the dead silence unique to the Tibetan Plateau had been restored. My spirits raised, I walked back and forth both inside and outside the stupa, hoping to find something, but finding nothing instead. My inspection complete, I returned to my original hiding position in an attempt to wait for the voices to reappear. Yet once my nerves had sufficiently unwound, an irresistible wave of fatigue washed over me and I fell to sleep right there in the cold night.

When I woke again the sun was already high in the sky. I ate a simple meal then got up to check the inside and outside of the stupa once again. The bright light of the day didn't reveal anything worth noting, and I still could not find any evidence for or against the existence of trapped spirits. The experience of the night had left me dizzy and weak: it was difficult to concentrate on searching every inch of the ancient tower and examining every trivial thing. Instead, I sat on top of the stone pile, trying to remember every single detail of the night's incidents in an attempt to dig out fresh discoveries. The many haunting sounds I had heard included chanting, screaming, shrieking, and other voices that clearly spilled from human lips, but I was still inclined to believe that the true source of these noises was not something conscious. Whatever created these cries had not reacted in any way to the noise I personally had made; it had continued unalterably in its cacophony like an announcement from an automated tape recorder. Furthermore, the source of the uproar simply had to be from somewhere within the stupa. There was a difference in volume when listening outside or inside the tower, and it was also possible that the circular wall of the stupa's interior was acting as an amplifier to any sound produced within.

Only now did I pay attention to the cairn that lay in the center of the stupa. I had already looked over the *doubeng* following my entry, but I had made only a cursory examination of its appearance and the stones exposed on the outermost side. Now some vague intuition whispered to me that a store of secrets was certainly buried beneath this pile of rocks. Ten feet in diameter and five feet high, the cairn was built in the shape of a regular cone above a flattened sphere. There was also an elegance in the manner the stones had been piled up on one another: staggered and stacked one by one with obvious and meticulous care — quite different from the haphazard mani heaps found outside in the Tibetan wilderness. I reached as high as I could and one-by-one tried to pull out those higher stones within my reach. To begin with, the way the stones were stacked made it difficult for me to remove them, and despite my efforts I was able to remove only a couple of rocks. Later, as the overall structure of the cairn loosened, some of the stones at the top began to fall down, the whole cairn looking like it might collapse. When I removed my fifth stone, one side of the cairn gave out a ringing noise as it sank, and I heard a dull thump like the sound of bricks falling from a significant height. As I continued to remove more stones, the banging of more rocks falling continued to sound until one side of the cairn collapsed completely into a hole below. A gasp of cold heavy air burst out of the ground, revealing a spacious underground entrance before my very eyes.

It was a square portal about four feet wide. The top of a stone staircase was exposed just below the entrance hole, meaning that my search had finally led to a break-through — a huge basement existed below the ancient stupa. The top of the stone staircase had a style similar to that of the megalithic foundations of the stupa's outside base, the two forming halves of a twin set, almost as if the giant boulders used to build the foundations had suddenly collapsed at the entrance. The staircase was built from those same well-chiseled cyclopean granite blocks, with steep steps much narrower and higher than those of a normal staircase. The steps were as severely worn as the floor of the stupa, but chiseled onto their surface the last vestiges of strange curves decorated with unknown meaning were barely visible. Down, down the deep staircase went, so that even with a flashlight I still could not see where it ended somewhere in that blurry darkness. I lit a handful of kindling and threw it down from where I stood, watching as the flames rolled down the stairs till they finally came to rest on one of the steps. The fire continued to burn for a long time before extinguishing itself, reassuring me that there was still enough oxygen in the basement below for a descent. I then yelled down the hole, hoping with

extreme apprehension to make myself known to anything that might be lurking in the darkness below. Only a
weak echo answered me, an echo that was overwhelmed
with silence once it faded away.

After much deliberation, I took a few tools from
my bag to aid me in my investigation and any unexpected circumstances that might occur. Switching on
my bright flashlight, I walked down into the darkness
of the unknown. Just a few feet into my descent the
heavy granite blocks that had formed the stupa's base
disappeared and were replaced by a vast, dark emptiness.
In vain I tried to use the light from my torch to estimate
the size of this space. With the light I could clearly see
that an enormous and flat stone wall stood just to my
right, but when I cast the flashlight to the left I could
not see anything at all, the light merely swallowed up
by the impenetrable gloom. Only when I waved the
torch to scan the room could I make out the occasional
pale illumination of dark and unimaginably large stone
pillars standing in the emptiness. This vast subterranean
world was filled with an eerie atmosphere and a silence
that was broken only by my slight footsteps and the
pounding of my heart. Darkness scattered before my
flashlight when I turned it to illuminate the downward
sloping path ahead, surrounding my body and drown-
ing me within. These unworldly sights inspired strange
illusions in my head, where I saw the gargantuan stone
staircase taking me out of the stupa and beyond the
foothill by the placid lake — far beyond this familiar
world and out into an endless void where only darkness
prevailed. Mercifully, this horrifying hallucination did
not last long, as after descending about fifty to sixty feet

I arrived at another wide, flat space of ground. Against my expectations, the ground here was not built from the large, flat granite blocks of the ancient stupa, but from flattened octagonal tiles of a much larger scale. The tiles were more worn than the granite boulders used on the staircase, suggesting that the steep granite steps behind me and the base of the tower connected to it were not in fact the oldest parts of the building. Long before primitive men had dragged those megalithic blocks here to build this tower, an even older race had built this magnificent and imposing structure. More mystifying was that there was no thick layer of dust to be found on the ground as one would expect; indeed, the floor looked like it had been freshly swept. This gave me a deep feeling of unease, but when I turned the flashlight to my right and looked at the large stone wall there, I felt an even more inconceivable sense of shock and confusion.

An arched doorway of incredible proportions was carved into the majestic high wall to my right. It must have been over thirty feet high and twenty feet wide, but had been blocked tight by large boulders of irregular shape. Irregular though they were, the boulders had been piled up in such a dense and compact manner that they completely filled the entire arch, plainly the result of meticulous planning and construction. The archway was well preserved due to the depths of where we were, so I could easily imagine how it must have originally appeared. There was no sign on the doorframe as to how the door could be opened, but there were some huge symbols like curved hieroglyphs. These symbols were totally different than any text system that I knew;

even somebody with my specialized background could scarcely classify them into any known linguistic family. The presence of this archway made me realize that I was not standing in a basement after all, but inside an enormous building that must have once stood upon the ground. For unknown reasons, something had sealed this entrance, perhaps even covering the whole thing in clay to conceal it entirely. Another possibility was the hill supporting the stupa had once been a burial mound, discovered by that later group of Neolithic ancestors who had built their huge granite tower over the majestic tomb. Then, as the years turned into centuries, a tribe of unknown Tibetans had stumbled upon the ruined granite tower and built a new stupa over the remains before disappearing for whatever mysterious reason. Finally, it was rediscovered by the cult mentioned in Tsesong Gyalpo's biography, who used it once more as a holy site until they were driven away by the son of the *tusi* and the stupa was sealed up and allowed to fall into silence again … until my arrival broke it.

After carefully reviewing the archway I turned to other places, allowing my torchlight to follow the tall smooth walls amidst the darkness as I tiptoed nervously forward from one area to another, hoping by this method to piece together a complete picture of the structure. Yet the more I learned about this building, the more confused and disturbed I felt. The interior of the room was a perfect octagonal shape with a diameter of about 150 feet. Identical archways of similar splendor were built into each of the eight monumental walls, and like the first archway I encountered they were all blocked with a mixture of large and small boulders. There were no visible traces of windows to be seen, most likely because the archways would have provided sufficient light during their heyday. The smooth flatness of the interior walls also seemed to indicate that they had once been painted or had large panels installed upon them. When I brushed against one of the walls I thought I was touching metal due to the cool smoothness, but when I knocked upon it, the sound was more like that of rock. Standing halfway between the walls and the center of the room were eight immense stone pillars supporting the roof of the structure. The pillars were smoothly polished and as thick as three people linking hands in a circle. The middle portion of the pillars was also thicker than the upper and lower ends, giving them an unusual bottle-shaped appearance. The colossal height of the room meant that the stone columns disappeared upward into the darkness where my torchlight could not reach, though I had caught a brief glimpse of the ceiling when I had descended the stone staircase. It was a vast and cleverly designed vault-shaped dome carved from titanic rocks. Beneath this cavernous roof and in the exact center of the building stood a strange square stone pillar, ten to fifteen feet tall, more than a foot wide, and engraved with weird curved abstract decorations on the upper end of each side. The curves were intricate and seemed to imply some form of mathematical design, but dissimilar to any symmetrical aesthetics that I was familiar with. Furthermore, the top of the stone column appeared to have something strange resting upon it. Due to the column's height I was unable to find a suitable angle to see exactly what it was, but from what I could just about see it seemed to be a highly unusual object composed of irregular polyhedron crystals.[14]

The light shining against the smooth wall revealed a host of bizarre and unique symbols and patterns. After closer inspection, I began to suspect that the similarly curved hieroglyphs I had seen on the archways were the language of the architects behind this building. I reasoned thus because the words occupied the most prominent position upon the wall, whereas their distribution elsewhere was more even. Yet what I could not understand was why these words had been carved ten to twenty feet high, as if giants had inscribed them. Alongside these words were many complex decorative patterns made up of alien curves that were impossible for me to decipher. Lower down there were other weird patterns and ciphers inscribed — those with similar characteristics often appearing next to one another. From this, I could easily determine how many races of differing cultures had passed through these walls. In total there were around six different groups of symbols, two of which I could state their origin with certainty. One set was composed of words and pictures left from the Tubo period, the other was from the Qing dynasty — most likely a remnant of that blasphemous religious sect. Unfortunately, the Tibetan words on the wall failed to reveal anything new to me; they only repeated that this building was "Sipasa" and that the wheel of

14   Lovecraft's "The Haunter of the Dark" may provide the interested reader with further background on what these crystals represent.

reincarnation was centered here. Elsewhere, I also found an engraving that proved to be an earlier version of Dawa Tsering's thangka, dating from the Tubo Kingdom. The content of the carving was almost identical to the thangka, though far richer in detail. At its center was an image of an octagon; however, eight smaller octagons surrounded this one. Of the different humans and monsters that appeared in the central octagon, one of each was then displayed in the separate surrounding octagons. For example, the small octagon on the upper right seemed to house a group of Tibetans; the lower left contained the anthropomorphized snake creatures; and the top center featured something like a sea anemone that I couldn't decide whether was plant or animal. I thought that engravings left here from other eras may have influenced these drawings; I had already seen some carvings of the snake creatures on the walls of the northeast corner. This situation had happened before in places such as the Mogao Caves,[15] which had a long history of being reused by subsequent cultures. As for those pictures whose origins I could not decipher — they were even more outlandish. The artists behind these engravings had symbolically portrayed themselves as various monsters. Some of the pictures showed a group of serpentine creatures finding the building for the first time — which back then stood alone on a wide plain. Other pictures had scenes of countless winged bat-like beasts worshipping the edifice as it towered above the

15   The Mogao Caves, also known as the Cave of a Thousand
      Buddhas, are a system of Buddhist caves situated in
      Dunhuang, Gansu Province.

treetops of a tropical jungle. Perhaps these creatures were the totem symbols of the various peoples who had left their mark on these walls. After all, the tradition of portraying humans as animals exists within many early civilizations, like the feathered serpents of the Aztecs or Manchurian shamans wrapped up in animal skins.

Other than the steep stone staircase I had come down and the eight blocked arches, there were no other exits in the building. This should have been the end of my exploration, but I still had no reasonable explanation for the ghastly sounds of the previous night. The space was devoid of any living thing, and I certainly had not seen any device that could have produced such grisly noise. However, I had already put all these questions at the back of my mind as all of my new discoveries had led me to forget my original purpose for entering this place, and the fear and unease I had felt before. I took many photos of the building and of those strange wall carvings, as well as making detailed records one by one. It was already late by the time I finished my work and returned to the surface via the stone steps; but after one taste of the bitterly cold night air I decided to avoid it by heading back down below to the basement. In hindsight, my sudden decision to spend the night alone in such a huge and unfathomable abyss — especially since nobody knew my whereabouts — was quite simply foolish. My senses had been distorted by the thrill of discovery. After hastily gobbling down some food, I unhesitatingly packed my belongings into my backpack and brought them all down to the cellar below.

I lit a small campfire in a corner of the basement by the staircase and resumed the work I had started during the day. The underground setting meant that the temperature was much more comfortable than the surface. After experiencing so many emotions through the day — apprehension, confusion, and excitement — a wave of exhaustion overpowered me. The debilitating effects of sleep deprivation from the previous night began to fade. Soon, I drifted asleep against the granite steps.

As for what happened next, I still cannot say exactly. Indeed, to this day I maintain hope that what I saw that night was nothing more than the strange by-product of fatigue, dank air, and altitude sickness. Now, in retrospect, everything was so against reason and so clouded in a fog of uncertainty that I question my own memory and its authenticity.

I remember that it was almost midnight when I awoke. Vague sounds began to make themselves known and gradually became louder, yet I did not feel the fear I had the day before. This time I was expecting the haunting cries. But when I looked around to find the source of the sound, I found myself petrified in one spot due to the astonishing scene that had appeared before me. It was a very simple sight, but one that defied all common sense and expectation, leading me to wonder if I was in fact still asleep. I have already mentioned that I had deliberately chosen to spend the night in this underground cavern so as to avoid the freezing temperatures that ravage the surface at night, and I have highlighted that the entire structure was lodged deep under the foothill except for the granite staircase that provided the only way out. Despite all this, a dim but ever-changing light was slowly increasing in strength, and this light was coming from those archways that had been blocked with rubble. This was no mere glimmer of phosphorescence leaking from the cracks between the rocks; no, it was a faint glow shining from the center of the archways themselves, shooting out and illuminating the titanic octagonal rock slabs on the ground. It was as if a door had been opened in a dark room as I saw the cold white light spilling out like water across the floor. Astonishingly, light was pouring in not only from the archway next to me but from *all* the archways, as if the stones that blocked the arches had disappeared or the building had once again risen to the surface where moonlight could flood in from the eight arches and dimly light the wide area.

As my eyes grew accustomed to the dull light, I began to become aware of the true appearance of this magnificent structure: an awareness that only served to plunge me into greater fear and anxiety. For the first time I clearly recognized the inhuman immensity of what I had stumbled upon; I had become Gulliver entering the land of Brobdingnag — as small and as insignificant as an ant in a room. Of even greater concern were the rays of light shining out from the arches. Their brightness fluctuated with great irregularity: extinguishing, fading, now a brilliant white.... I found it unutterably grotesque. Reason urged me to flee from that place lest I encounter something that would leave me forever unable to return to the outside world with my sanity intact. Resist as I tried, the light seemed to contain an inexorable magic. I found myself unwillingly pulled up to my feet then marching mechanically forward, eager to see what lay behind the arches. The nearest arch was less than ten feet away, but it felt like I had walked for an hour before

I finally arrived and nervously brought my head close to the wall. I have no idea how to describe what I saw next.

Countless strange and chaotic visions rushed simultaneously into my field of vision. I saw a dense jungle of thickly stemmed ferns as tall as trees. I saw a forsaken desert spread out beneath the pale moonlight, the remains of dark gigantic buildings scattered across it. A majestic city built from every kind of towering spire. Rolling hills half covered in cloud … dark stalactite caves glowing with alien fluorescence … clouds evaporating … the vast dark ocean and rocky beaches smothered in seaweed. They were like apparitions superimposed upon one another, but each image was truly incomparable on its own. Like a mad, spinning kaleidoscope, the reverse side of the archway brought endless new vistas toward my eyes before they dissipated and were lost within the chaos of other visions. Occasionally I could see the giant rocks that should have been blocking the arch, but they seemed different from the ones I had first seen. The vistas that appeared in the archway all seemed to have been observed from the point of view of the stupa, though the location of the stupa differed from scene to scene. Some of the sights revealed within the arch could have been taken only from the vantage point of a steep mountain slope, whereas others faced boundless deserts and plains. Some must have even shown underground grottoes, since I could see complex cave systems covered in numerous holes and glowing with faint luminosity. These illusions did not present themselves like drawings on a flat scroll; they more resembled an immense world of images stacked one atop the other, spreading out from the stupa, revealing ever more wondrous and indescribable scenes every time I moved my eyes. Yet I knew that this could only be an illusory fantasy, for when I reached out my hand in fascination to grasp the strange world that existed beyond the arch, I could feel only those huge stones trapped within. They were still there as before — blocking the archway — merely enshrouded by a cloak of phantasms.

The varied scenes all changed at different speeds. While some scenes seemed to condense thousands of years into a fast-forwarded movie, others were shown at a normal pace or even near-solidified clips of utter meaninglessness. Within these images, I saw ghostly jungles of innumerable weird plants flourishing under a sky of surging whitewater vapor that then withered and degenerated into a vast and sinister swamp. Piece by piece the swamp dried up, retreating in the face of an encroaching desert of dry pebbles. Then it became lush again, a large cluster of fresh plants forming a new forest of verdant green out of the air. I saw an infinite expanse of lofty mountains transform itself into a vast and gloomy ocean, and the rolling waves of that same ocean recede against the formation of a new land. I saw giant glaciers of blue and white coming and going, covering everything near and far in a sheet of white snow, competing for space against tall cascading coniferous forests. I saw immeasurable numbers of towering incomparable buildings, piled up like children's building blocks, rising from a dense jungle until they entered the unseen outer limits of the sky. The sky-scraping towers then collapsed, leaving behind corpses of giant stones half-hidden in the yellow desert sands. Eventually, they disappeared totally from my vision, replaced by new buildings erected on the ground where they once stood; buildings that prospered and flourished and then collapsed and disappeared again. I saw countless such reincarnations: each city comparable to our bustling modern metropolises — actually much more magnificent than our puny urban dwellings — but none of them escaped their ultimate fate. Each city would eventually collapse into ruin, either to be consumed by the desert or replaced by a new city. It never stopped.

With further examination, I slowly realized that these staggered scenes were connected to one another. A vista of grassland would imperceptibly evolve into a mountain range that I had previously seen, and the same deserts and oceans would reappear in the same place millions of years later. From this uncanny coincidence I began to get the strange intuition that all of these scenes were related. Perhaps they all reflected the same image of a certain location over the course of its long history, but for some unknown reason split into lots of separate clips, then stacked together and revealed to me. I had no way of knowing exactly what the images reflected, though perhaps they symbolized the changes the stupa had undergone throughout its long history. This, however, seemed unlikely, because if it was true then the history of the octagonal building went far beyond even the most absurd conjectures somebody could make.

Apart from the rapidly changing scenes, the normal-paced and near-static images were equally confusing — not to mention horrifying and disturbing. Since the changes within these apparitions were not as fast-paced or jumpy as the other visions, they provided a good opportunity to take a deeper look at their details. Yet the closer I looked at those images, the more incredulous and disturbed I became. These scenes were filled with all types and kinds of monstrosity that had never been included in any fossil record or archaeological book. The creatures slithered, shambled, and flapped in their respective worlds, committing the most unmentionable acts. I would say that several of them resembled the strange patterns featured in the unusual thangka and the Tubo engravings, but in truth they more closely resembled the twisted nightmares of the deranged.

I saw rainbow-colored cone-shaped creatures — ten feet high — they stretched out the four thick appendages that grew from the tops of their cones beneath the shade of tall thick ferns. Surprisingly, they slithered leisurely around their cyclopean stone city in a manner possible only by intelligent creatures. In another scene, a horde of gargantuan bat-like black-snouted winged creatures careened across the sky in droves toward the distant mountains. I also witnessed a tribe of speckle-scaled snakes, clothed in bizarre and outlandish costumes, possessed of arms and legs and standing upright. Out of the tall dark coniferous forest they filed, slowly and gently winding over the vast hillside beside the archway, till they faced my direction and began to worship. Then, in an enormous cavern that branched into a myriad of complex smaller caves, I saw several bronze-colored men wearing strange robes and jewelry. They were certainly not Tibetan. Fearfully they were placing large boulders within the arches, blocking them up, while standing behind them were monsters that I cannot even bring myself to describe. The monsters passed the enormous megalithic boulders one by one to the men's waiting hands. When I dared to peek again at the following scene, I saw a swarm of horrific Coleoptera beetles — almost as big as men — removing the blocks, revealing a white city atop a vast plain. I saw so many strange creatures and humans, living like modern-day man in their own little worlds, and also disappearing forever alongside those worlds.[16]

Vivid and lifelike though the scenes were, and certainly enough to subvert all knowledge of geological history known today, I must admit that I had no doubt these were nothing more than hallucinations brought on by altitude sickness and fatigue. The inhuman size and solidity of this building had led my tired brain to conjure up these various and incomparably eccentric cities. In all likelihood the thangka and the Tubo wall engravings had birthed those monsters within my imagination and placed them one by one into different imaginary scenes to form one vivid illusion. What else could it be? Had I really seen the long history of this building — a history far beyond most people's imagination? Had this building really stood here back in the days when our mammalian ancestors still fled in fear from reptilian giants?

Another scene appeared to burden my already shattered nerves. Wriggling by me, beneath a canopy of dark-green feathered fern leaves, was one of the tall

16  Those eager to learn more about the creatures described should read Lovecraft's *The Shadow Out of Time* and "The Haunter of the Dark."

anemone-like creatures with the four thick appendages that I had seen previously. However, it did not stop in front in the archway, nor did it suddenly disappear. Instead, I saw it walk directly into the archway and pass through the illusion-covered stone wall like a ghost, though in reality it remained within the arch. I watched as the huge multi-colored cone passed by my side, squirming its way toward the center of the building, its stout tentacles above its oscillating body seemingly pausing for a moment in my direction. My gaze followed its immense body gradually move into the building, and then I beheld the most horrifying sight of all.

Since my attention had been focused on the intricate psychedelic landscape beyond the arch, I had not noticed the changes in the ghostly sounds I had heard earlier. They had become extremely loud and chaotic. It was not until my eyes turned back to the building's interior that I finally realized the origin of those sounds: the center of this majestic building was now filled with a large number of the monsters that had appeared in those strange scenes! Two or three of the large cone creatures surrounded the building's central column and appeared to be fiddling with the strange crystal on top of it. A larger group of humans dressed in the Tibetan style, kneeling alongside the serpentine monsters, were scattered in the farther outreaches of the room, chanting in joint worship. Near the top of the building, where the weak light failed to illuminate, I sensed an enormous creature creeping and climbing in the shadows — quietly lurking with only the occasional ghastly sound. Other monsters and people gathered by the surrounding archways, looking through them as I also had done.

What happened next brought my panicked nerves to an unprecedented climax. I only remember screaming with uncontrollable fear, fleeing back up the stone staircase on my hands and feet, and as I reached the final step that would allow me to escape this nightmarish abyss a certain thought grabbed a hold of me like an invisible pair of hands around my neck, choking me from screaming once more. This was my breaking point. After that, all I can recollect is running endlessly in the dark until I fell exhausted to the ground, into a coma of endless horrific nightmares.

The doctor related all of the following to me. Later that morning, several herdsmen found me lying insensate on the rock-strewn shore of Rongpo Tso. They carried me to the village of Chaba Gangca, where I was then transferred to the town hospital. Fortunately, apart from physical exhaustion and a mild fever, there wasn't anything seriously wrong with me. For five days I stayed in the simple town hospital and endured the combined torture of both psychological and physical suffering. Since I had lost my belongings and camera during my flight through the wilderness, I could not confide any of my experiences to others because I could not even be sure that what had happened that night was indeed cruel reality or nothing more than a terrible dream. When I was notified on the sixth day that I could leave the hospital, despite my weak condition I immediately boarded a car to Xining then booked the first flight home. Although it was a rush, my only wish at the time was to leave that land as soon as possible and block it from my sight and memory forever.

As for what transpired during the climax of my terror,

to this day I still feel as though it was all a dream. Events happened so suddenly, and due to my severe panic there are still some ambiguities and blanks in my recollection. As I said before, I watched as a large crowd of abominations emerged into the building from their various illusory dreamscapes and began to perform all manner of strange movements. No doubt that your thoughts upon seeing them for the first time would have been the same as mine: that they were merely solitary apparitions or perhaps the remnants of past incidents that had somehow ingrained themselves upon this building for unknown reasons. Maybe this was even the true source of those ancient trapped souls as told in the ghost stories. Petrified, I watched as the creatures interacted with one another, and I quickly realized that these phantoms were not in fact independent from one another, but were actually all part of the same gigantic scene. Using their sturdy tentacles, the huge cone-shaped beings attempted to drive away the surrounding serpentine creatures, whilst other members of the snake-men seemed to be communicating with the men dressed as Tibetans. At the same time, other Tibetans were repelling winged monsters that crept down from the colossal stone pillars.

It was then that I saw a middle-aged man dressed in luxurious Tibetan costume running to me in horror. From his attire — expensive furs, opulently ornate robes, a decorative gold-sheathed dagger — he looked to be a noble from the Ming or Qing dynasty. Suddenly, the most unexpected thing happened: this apparition tightly grasped my arm like a real person. I could clearly feel his two warm hands gripping my arm with great force and fear, so strongly that it hurt me. I could even smell the faint scent of unique spices as once used by Tibetan aristocracy. He spoke to me — his words different than the modern Tibetan language that I was familiar with, but I could still understand one or two simple words.

"Help me ..." he whispered.

A vast black shadow then descended from the sky, silently dragging him away in the blink of an eye to the dark eaves on high before he could even scream. Then another claw grabbed my arm from behind. I did not know what it was as I did not dare to look back, but those thin bony talons could not have belonged to any normal human being. I screamed out in fright, desperately pulling myself free from the clutch of those claws, and then fled up the steep stone staircase. As I reached the final few steps, fate once again revealed its cruel face, and a horrifying realization shattered my last remaining senses — pushing me over into an abyss of madness. I could not breathe; only my fearful instincts drove me forward, pushing me to leave forever that place that could exist only in nightmares.

Though ridiculous and contrary to all known reason and logic, my clear and simple realization at that moment was faultless. As I fled, it dawned on me that the bloodcurdling scream I had heard the night before was none other than my own.

*The End*

The Anthropologist had related his story admirably, though he was painfully ignorant as to the reality of what he had actually encountered. What an accursed waste that the privilege of peering through the window of time and space, of gazing into the reachless corners of the universe's secrets past and to come, had been bestowed upon one oblivious to the maddening infinity of the cosmos. Varied shapes of life had dragged out their multimillenial courses on the planet's age-racked surface before his very eyes, but for all the knowledge it had imparted he might have well as been staring into a child's kaleidoscope or some other such juvenile toy.

"Do you know what I saw?" asked the Anthropologist. "Do you know what those creatures were?"

I considered for a moment whether or not to answer his question. Should I shatter this already fragile mind with the truth of the Serpent-Men of fabled Valusia and the black-snouted winged creatures that slithered and flew across this world long before man's ancestors had climbed down from the trees, not to mention the cold-blooded beetles who will one day build their civilization atop the ruins of the long-forgotten human race, or the Great Race who travel from eon to eon? To do so would only be a cruelty, like whispering of death to a newborn.

"There are many species other than man that have passed through the Tibetan Plateau, and many more still to come," was all I was willing to offer. "The arc of history runs long."

The Anthropologist pondered this for a moment. "I have heard of strange creatures during my research. The Tibetans speak of the Mi-Go, a race of abominable snowmen or yetis that haunt the lonely Himalayan mountain tops."

"Oh, is that so?" I smiled, or did my closest approximation of a smile.

The Anthropologist continued in his witless speculations about Outer Ones and Wild Men. I chose to cease listening, as there was nothing he could teach me in this regard. Instead, I rolled up the thangka and placed it carefully back in the box alongside the other curios.

"Wait!" cried the Researcher. "You promised we could leave!"

"Yes, you gave your word!" chimed in the Historian.

I closed the box, making sure that it was locked and secure for the long journey ahead. The last thing I desired after such effort in gathering these artefacts and learning their stories would be to lose them halfway on my journey home. The box secured, I turned once again to my four guests and addressed them.

"And leave we shall. We leave immediately. It will be a long and cold journey, but you will not come to any harm. You will feel nothing in your containers. You will be perfectly safe. All four of you have been lucky enough to be afforded glimpses into the unknown. Few such as you have had the chance to gaze into those mysteries that man has striven in vain to fathom. Yet luckier still are you, for the universe has more mysteries to share with you, and I shall guide you to them."

སྤྲང་པ

"What do you mean?" exclaimed the Dreamer. "Where are we going?"

Yet I did not answer the Dreamer, nor would he have heard me even if I had, for I had already unplugged the sockets to his container that gave him sensory awareness of sight, sound, and speech. The Dreamer disconnected, I then walked behind the other three cylinders containing my guests, removing their only access to the outside world. The strange vibrations that had reverberated during our narrations suddenly came to a cease. I allowed my fungoid claw to linger over their ether-tight cylinders; their disembodied brains floating peacefully within — immersed in a viscous fluid — now deprived of all corporeal perception till I chose to reconnect them for the benefit of my fellow beings.

Holding the box in one claw, and strapping the four containers across me in a belt specially tailored to this purpose, I stepped out into the night air and allowed the cold wind to wash over me. I stretched out my membranous wings, looking up into the vast infinity of space toward the direction of Yuggoth — that strangely organized abyss wholly beyond the utmost reach of any human imagination. I had been away too long, for I yearned for its black rivers of pitch that flow beneath cyclopean bridges and for its great terraced stone towers that loom above fungoid gardens and windowless cities. To nighted Yuggoth we would go, where these storytellers would recite their stories again and again in lightless rooms for our entertainment and education for all eternity.

My antennas bristled in the cooling wind of the dead of night. Without further hesitation, I launched myself from the top of a bald, lonely hill, vanishing in the sky as my *great flapping wings were silhouetted for just an instant against the soft glow of the full moon.*